THIS COMIC
BELONGS TO:

Disney Vampirina

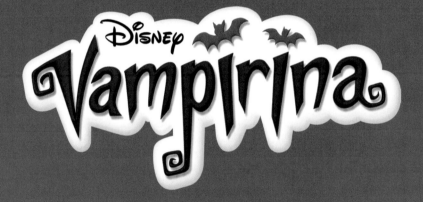

Published simultaneously in the United States and Canada by Joe Books Ltd,
489 College Street, Suite 203, Toronto, ON M6G 1A5.

www.joebooks.com

First Joe Books edition: November 2017

Print ISBN: 978-1-77275-559-6
ebook ISBN: 978-1-77275-856-6

Library and Archives Canada Cataloguing in Publication
information is available upon request.

Printed and bound in Canada
1 3 5 7 9 10 8 6 4 2

The Sleepover

CINESTORY COMIC

JOE BOOKS LTD

MEET VAMPIRINA AND HER FANGTASTIC FRIENDS & FAMILY!

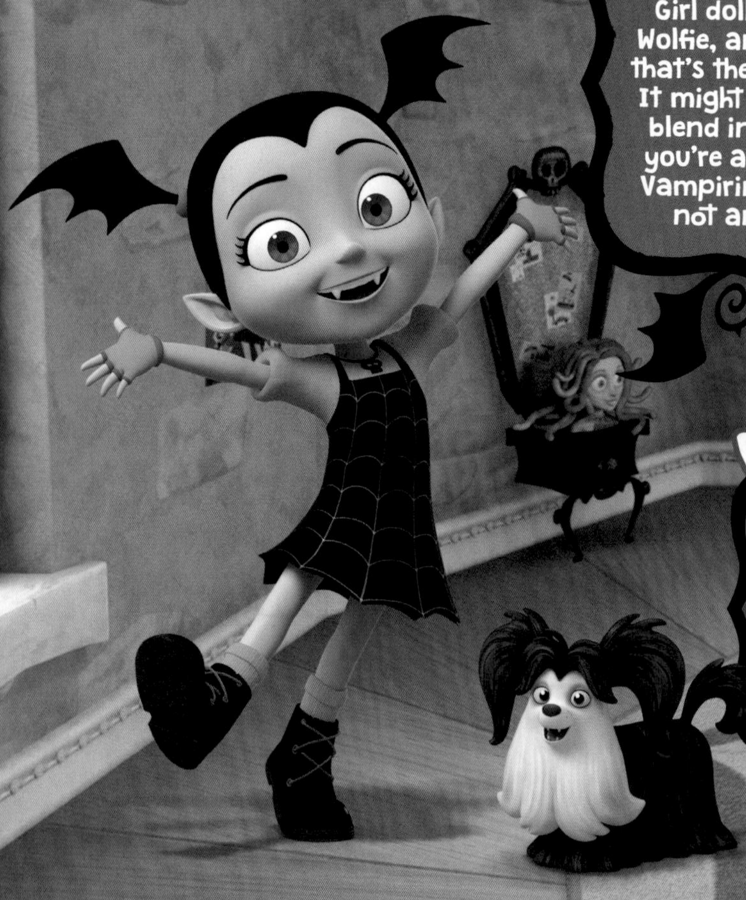

VAMPIRINA HAUNTLEY

Vampirina loves dancing, her Scream Girl dolls, her dog, Wolfie, and anything that's the color black. It might be easier to blend in, but when you're as unique as Vampirina is, that's not an option!

WOLFIE

Wolfie is the cutest little dog...except when there's a full moon out. Then, he's less like a sweet, little lapdog and more like a big, goofy werewolf.

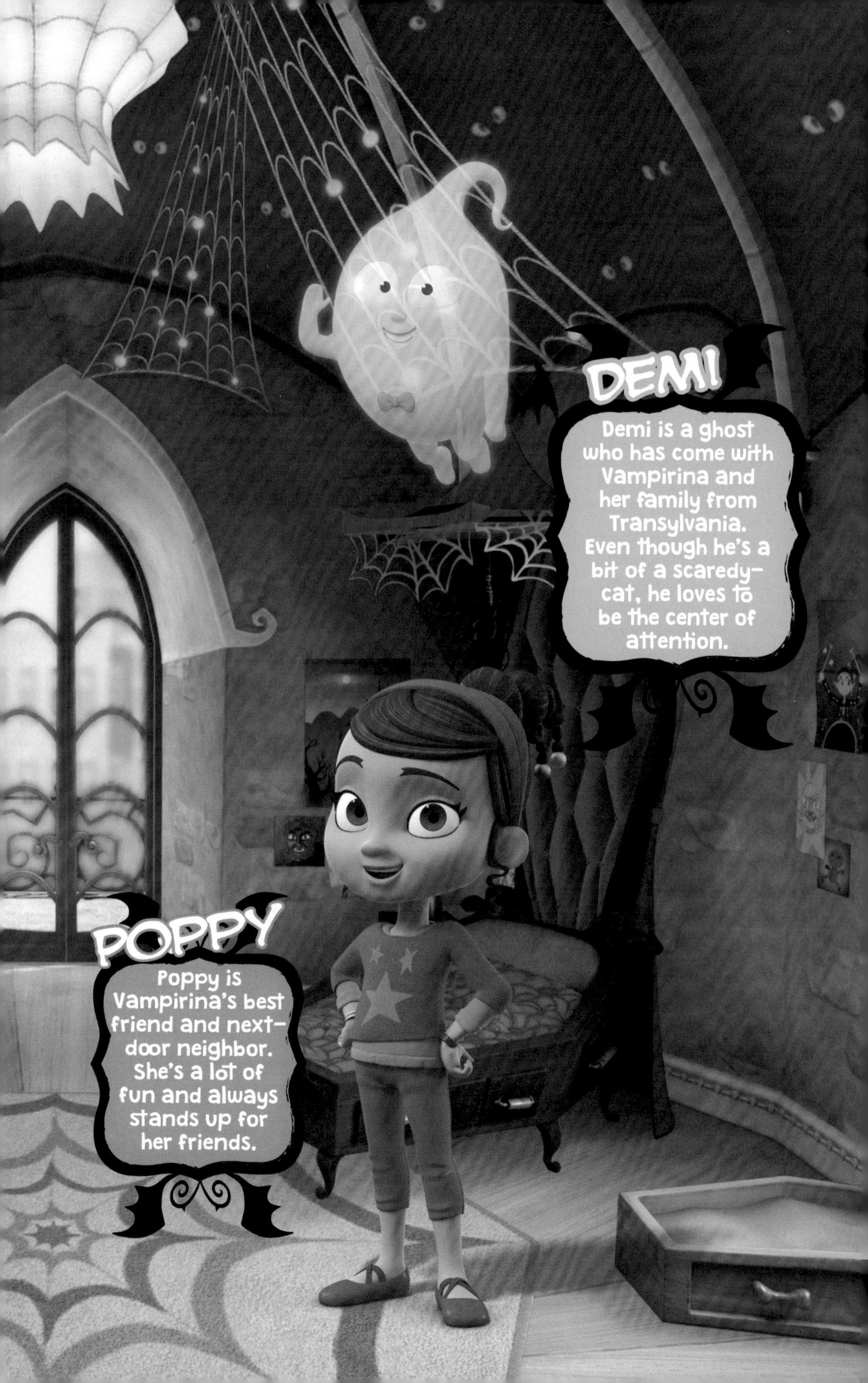

DEMI

Demi is a ghost who has come with Vampirina and her family from Transylvania. Even though he's a bit of a scaredy-cat, he loves to be the center of attention.

POPPY

Poppy is Vampirina's best friend and next-door neighbor. She's a lot of fun and always stands up for her friends.

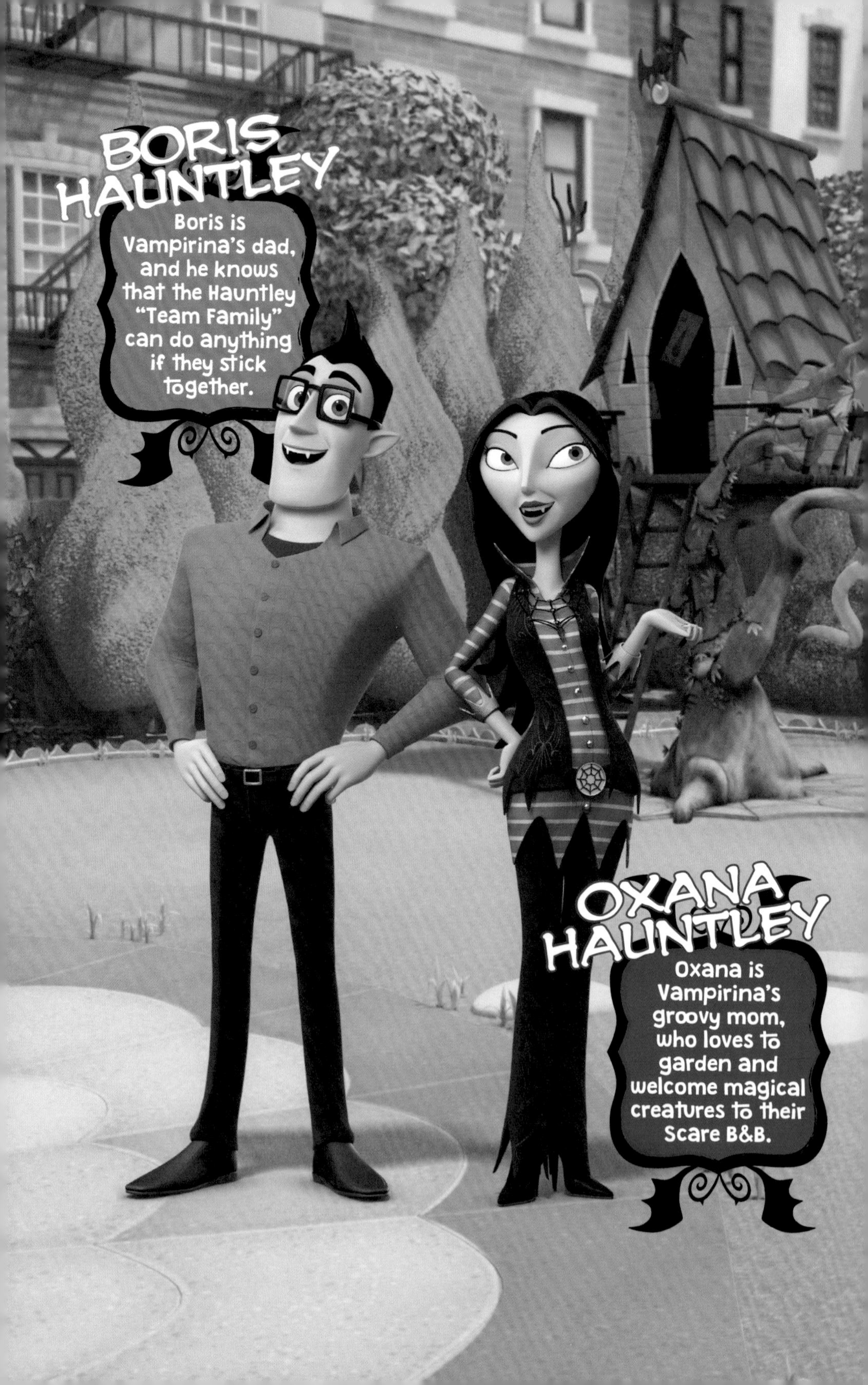
BORIS HAUNTLEY
Boris is Vampirina's dad, and he knows that the Hauntley "Team Family" can do anything if they stick together.
OXANA HAUNTLEY
Oxana is Vampirina's groovy mom, who loves to garden and welcome magical creatures to their Scare B&B.

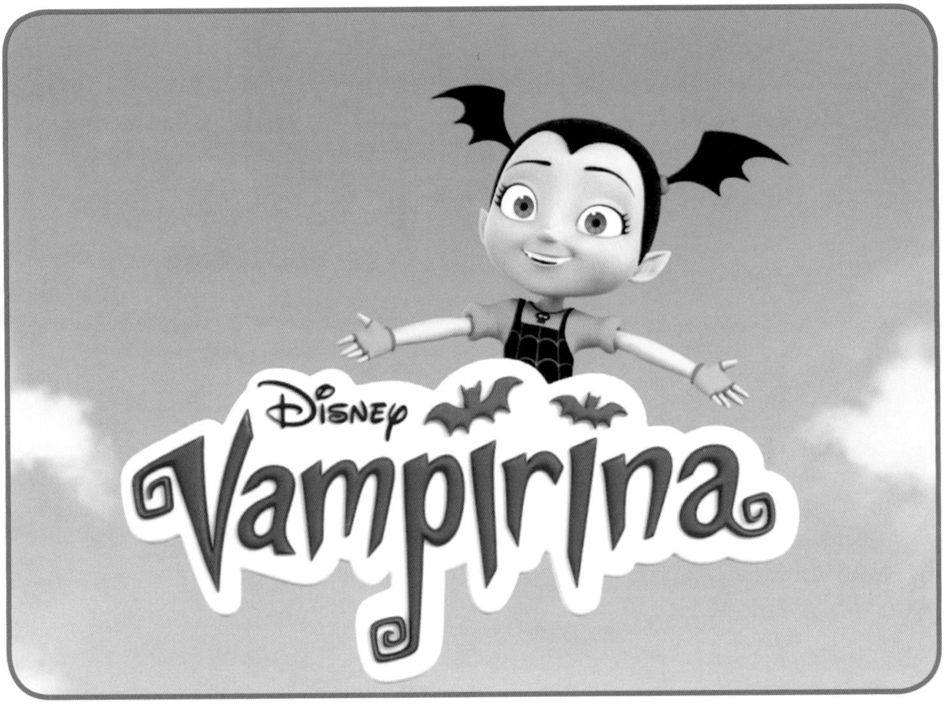
DISNEY
Vampirina

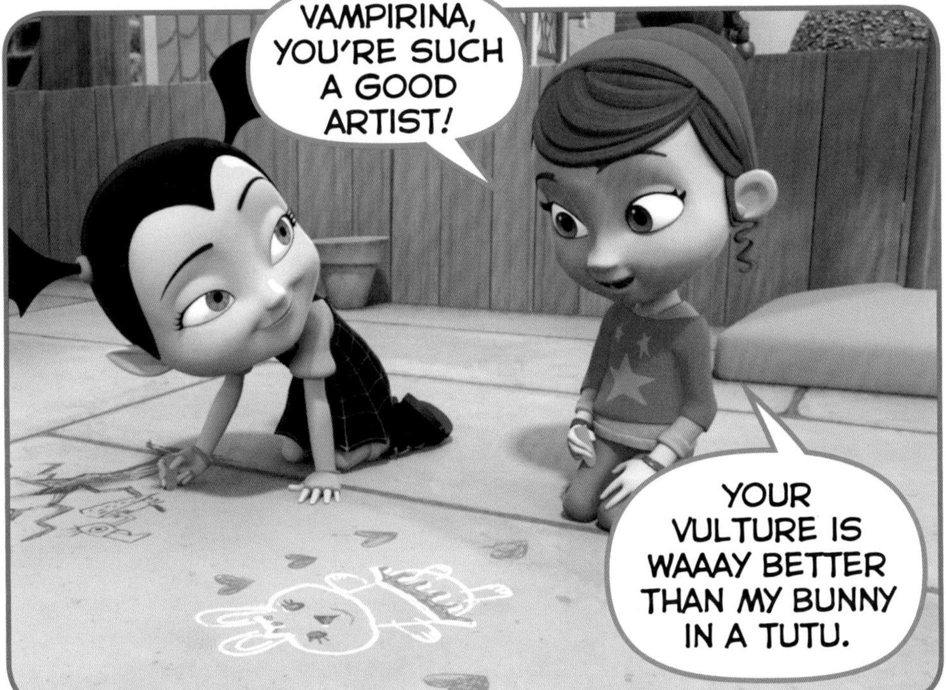
VAMPIRINA, YOU'RE SUCH A GOOD ARTIST!
YOUR VULTURE IS WAAAY BETTER THAN MY BUNNY IN A TUTU.

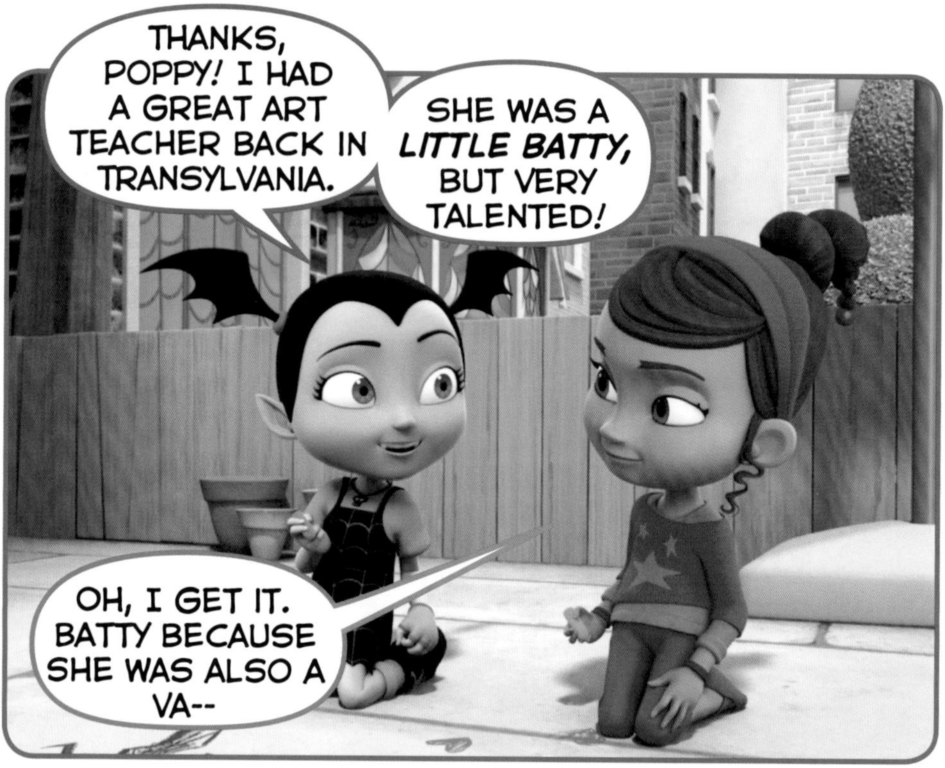
THANKS, POPPY! I HAD A GREAT ART TEACHER BACK IN TRANSYLVANIA.
SHE WAS A *LITTLE BATTY*, BUT VERY TALENTED!
OH, I GET IT. BATTY BECAUSE SHE WAS ALSO A VA--

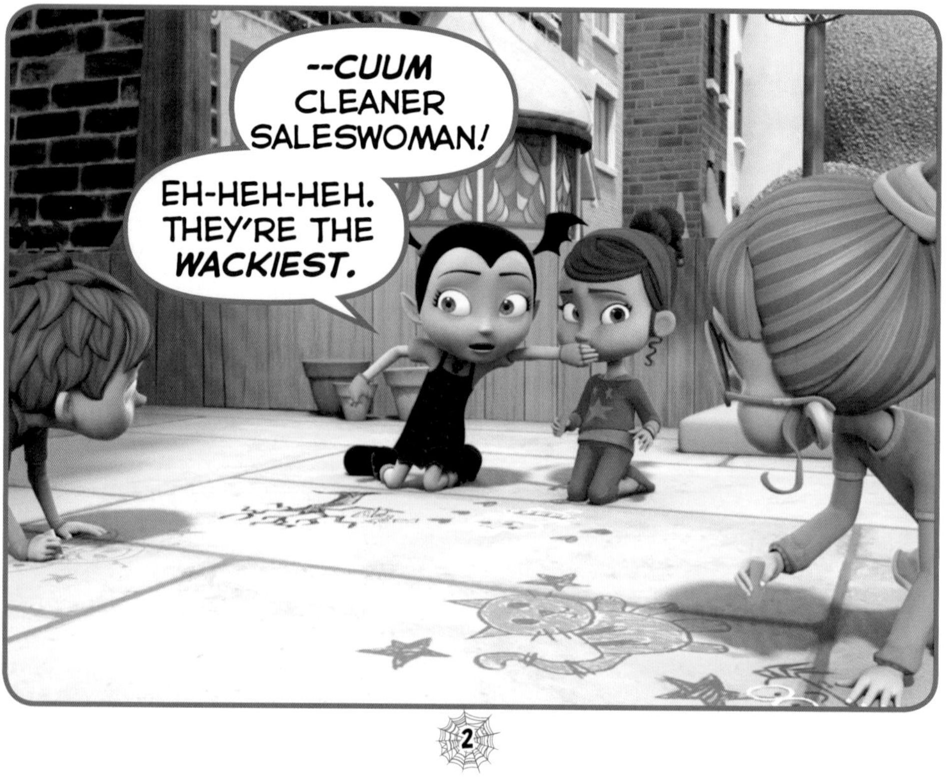
--*CUUM* CLEANER SALESWOMAN!
EH-HEH-HEH. THEY'RE THE *WACKIEST*.

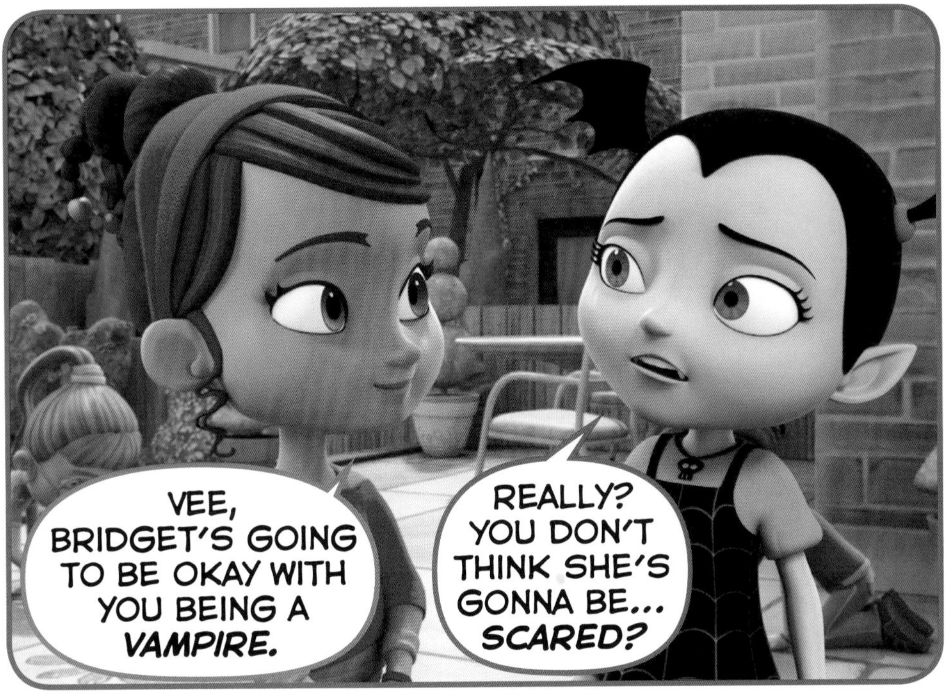
VEE, BRIDGET'S GOING TO BE OKAY WITH YOU BEING A *VAMPIRE.*
REALLY? YOU DON'T THINK SHE'S GONNA BE... *SCARED?*

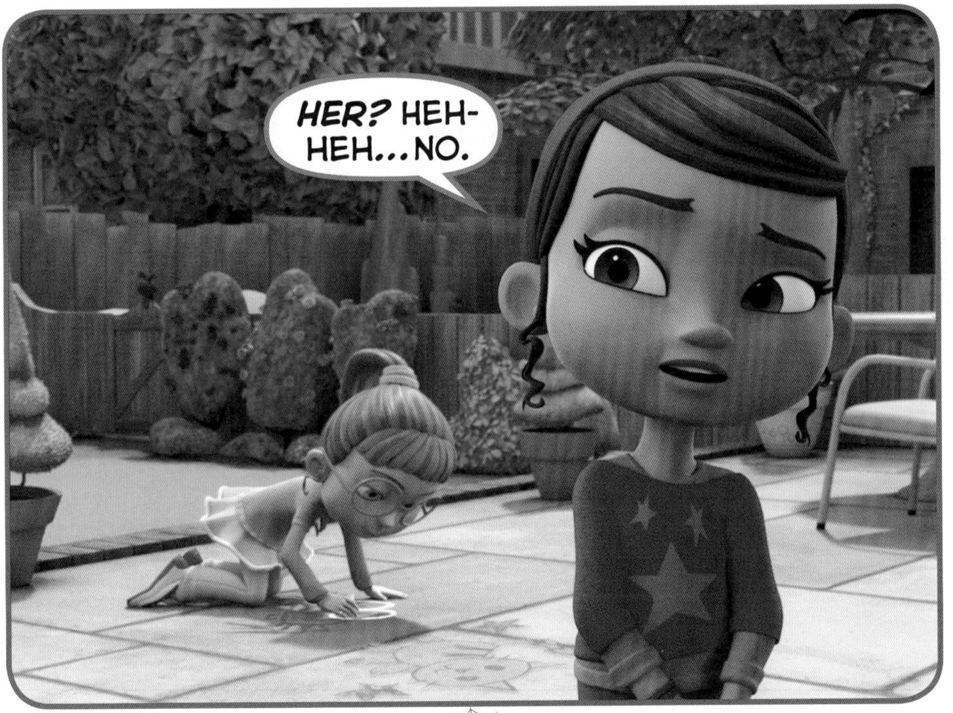
HER? HEH-HEH...NO.

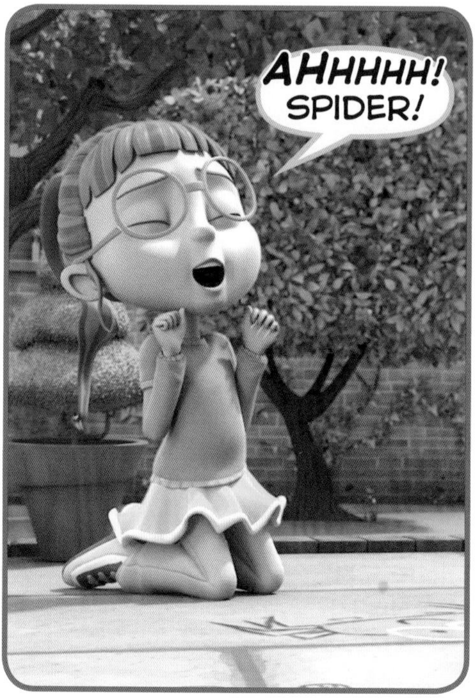
AHHHHH! SPIDER!

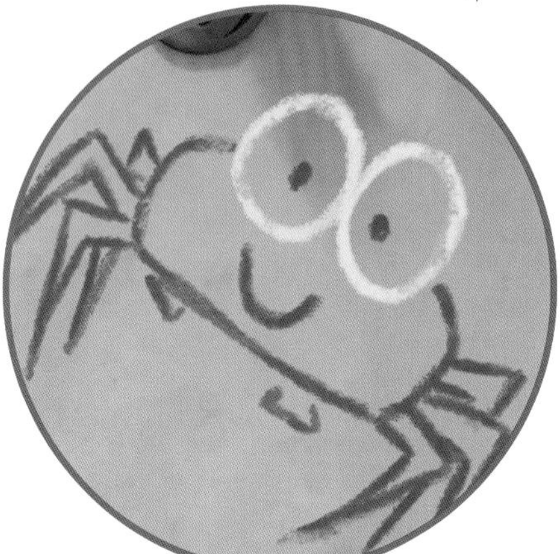

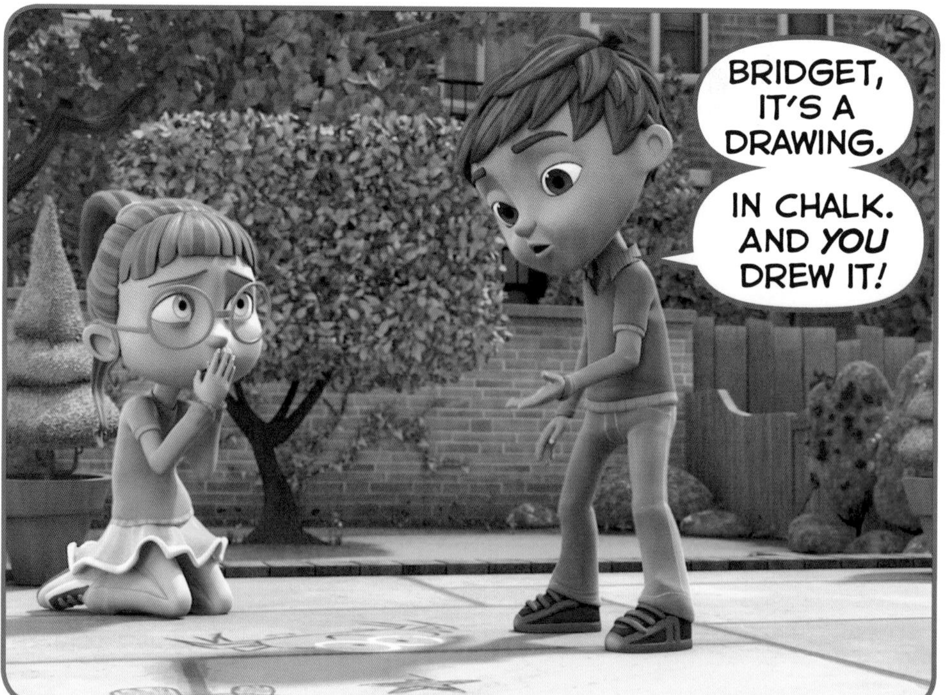
BRIDGET, IT'S A DRAWING.
IN CHALK. AND *YOU* DREW IT!

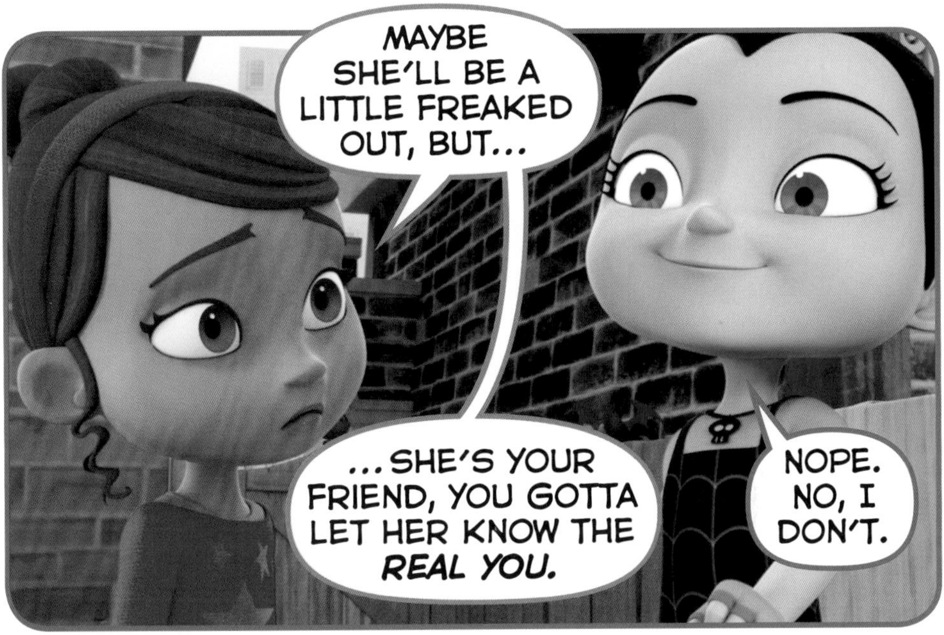
MAYBE SHE'LL BE A LITTLE FREAKED OUT, BUT...
...SHE'S YOUR FRIEND, YOU GOTTA LET HER KNOW THE *REAL YOU.*
NOPE. NO, I DON'T.

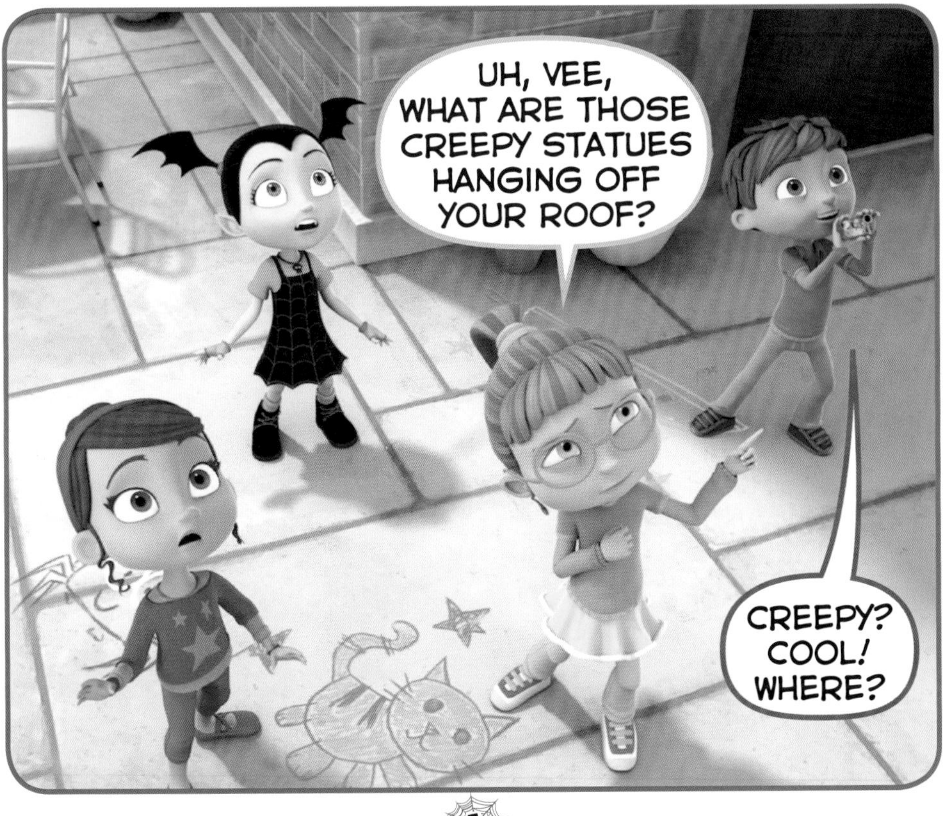
UH, VEE, WHAT ARE THOSE CREEPY STATUES HANGING OFF YOUR ROOF?
CREEPY? COOL! WHERE?

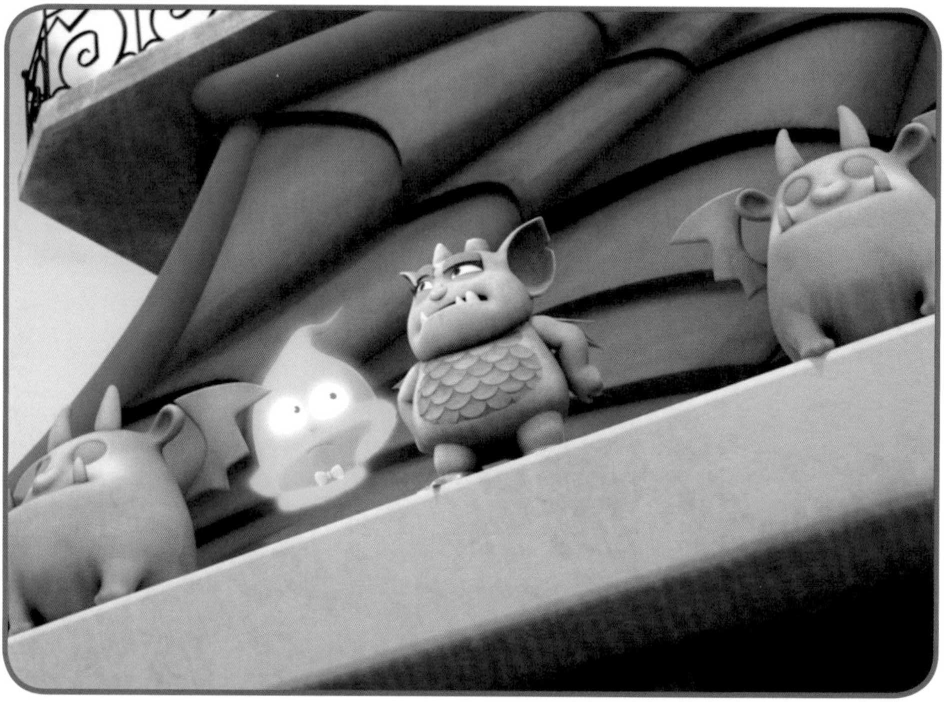

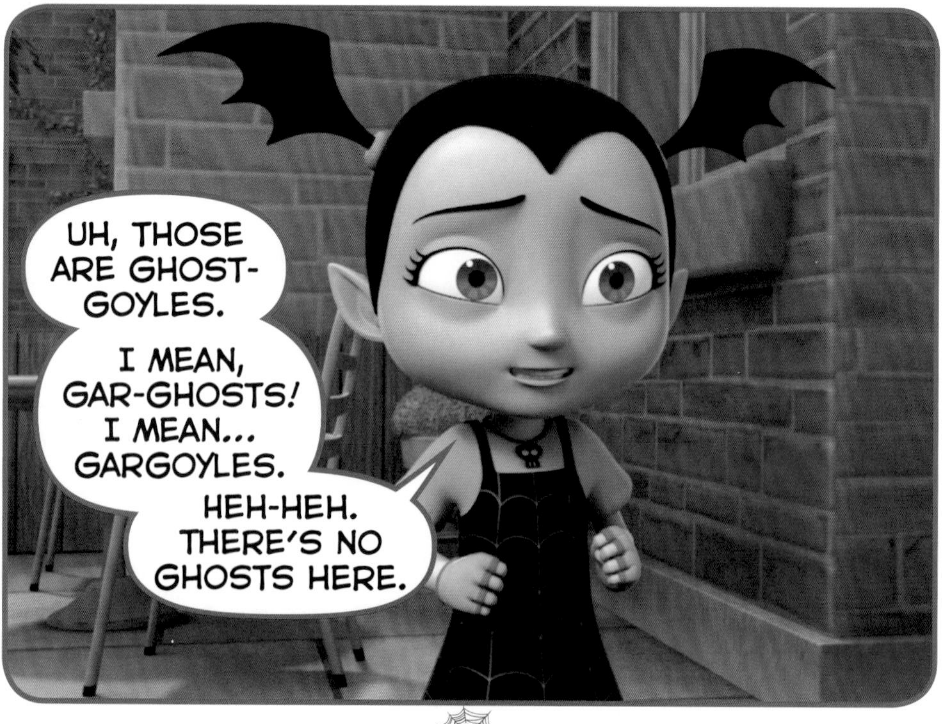
UH, THOSE ARE GHOST-GOYLES.
I MEAN, GAR-GHOSTS! I MEAN... GARGOYLES.
HEH-HEH. THERE'S NO GHOSTS HERE.

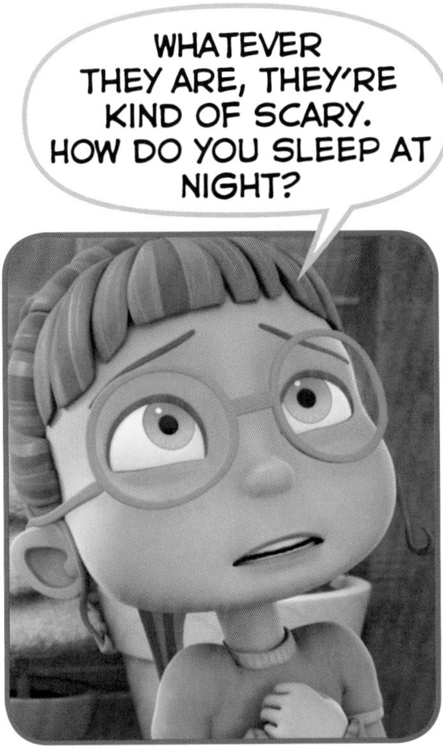
WHATEVER THEY ARE, THEY'RE KIND OF SCARY. HOW DO YOU SLEEP AT NIGHT?

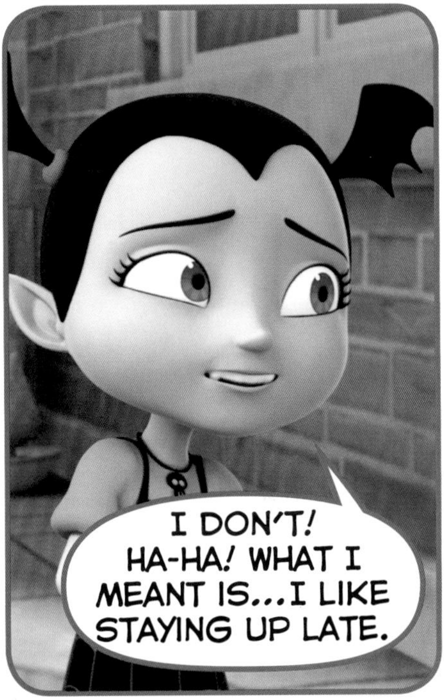
I DON'T! HA-HA! WHAT I MEANT IS...I LIKE STAYING UP LATE.

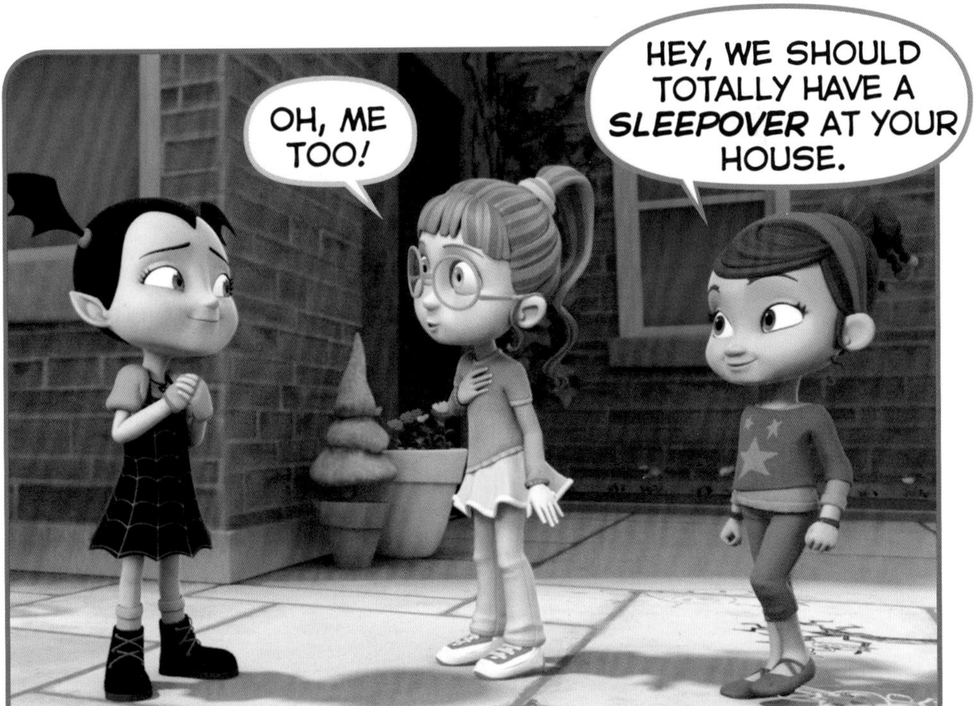
OH, ME TOO!
HEY, WE SHOULD TOTALLY HAVE A *SLEEPOVER* AT YOUR HOUSE.

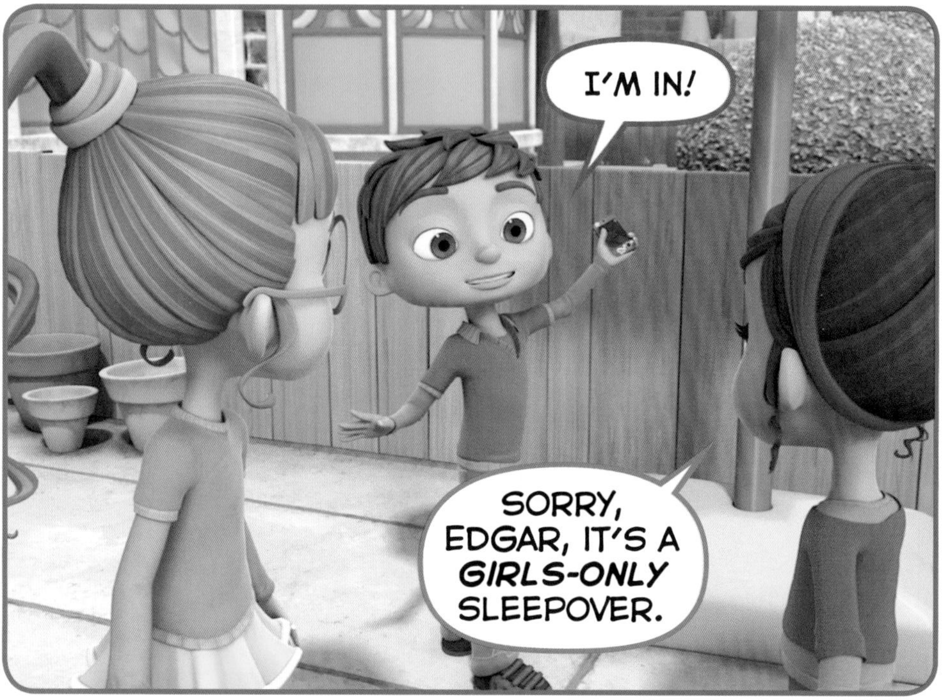
I'M IN!
SORRY, EDGAR, IT'S A *GIRLS-ONLY* SLEEPOVER.

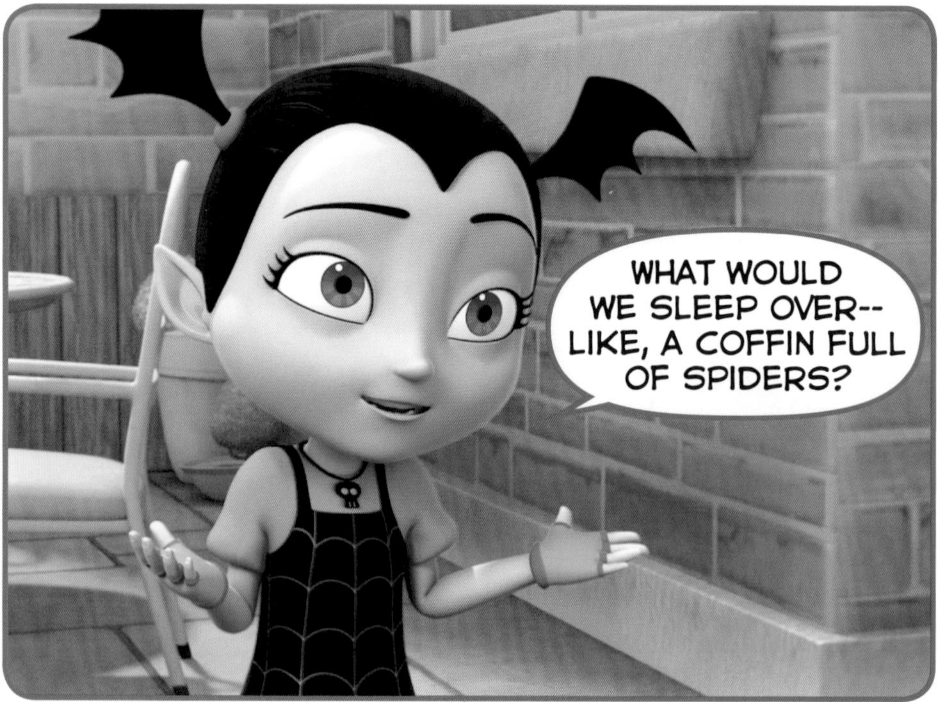
WHAT WOULD WE SLEEP OVER-- LIKE, A COFFIN FULL OF SPIDERS?

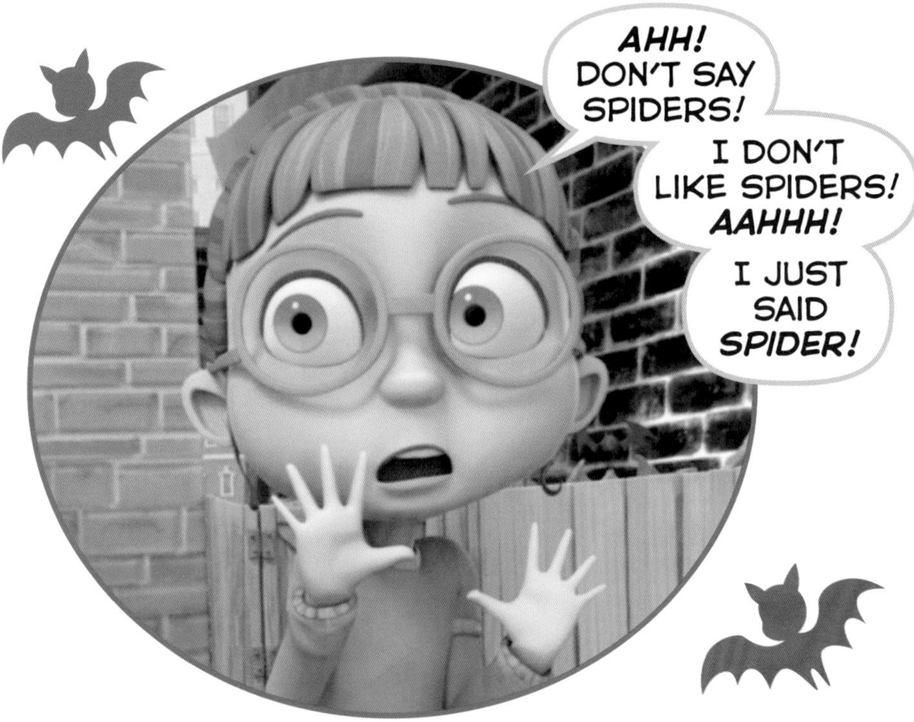
AHH! DON'T SAY SPIDERS!
I DON'T LIKE SPIDERS! AAHHH!
I JUST SAID SPIDER!

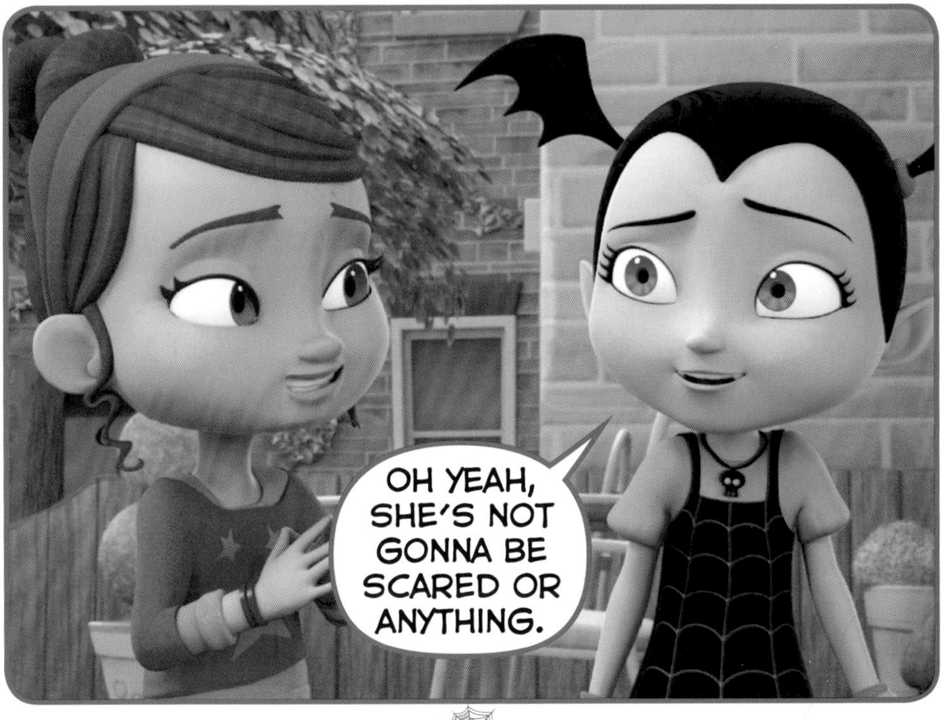
OH YEAH, SHE'S NOT GONNA BE SCARED OR ANYTHING.

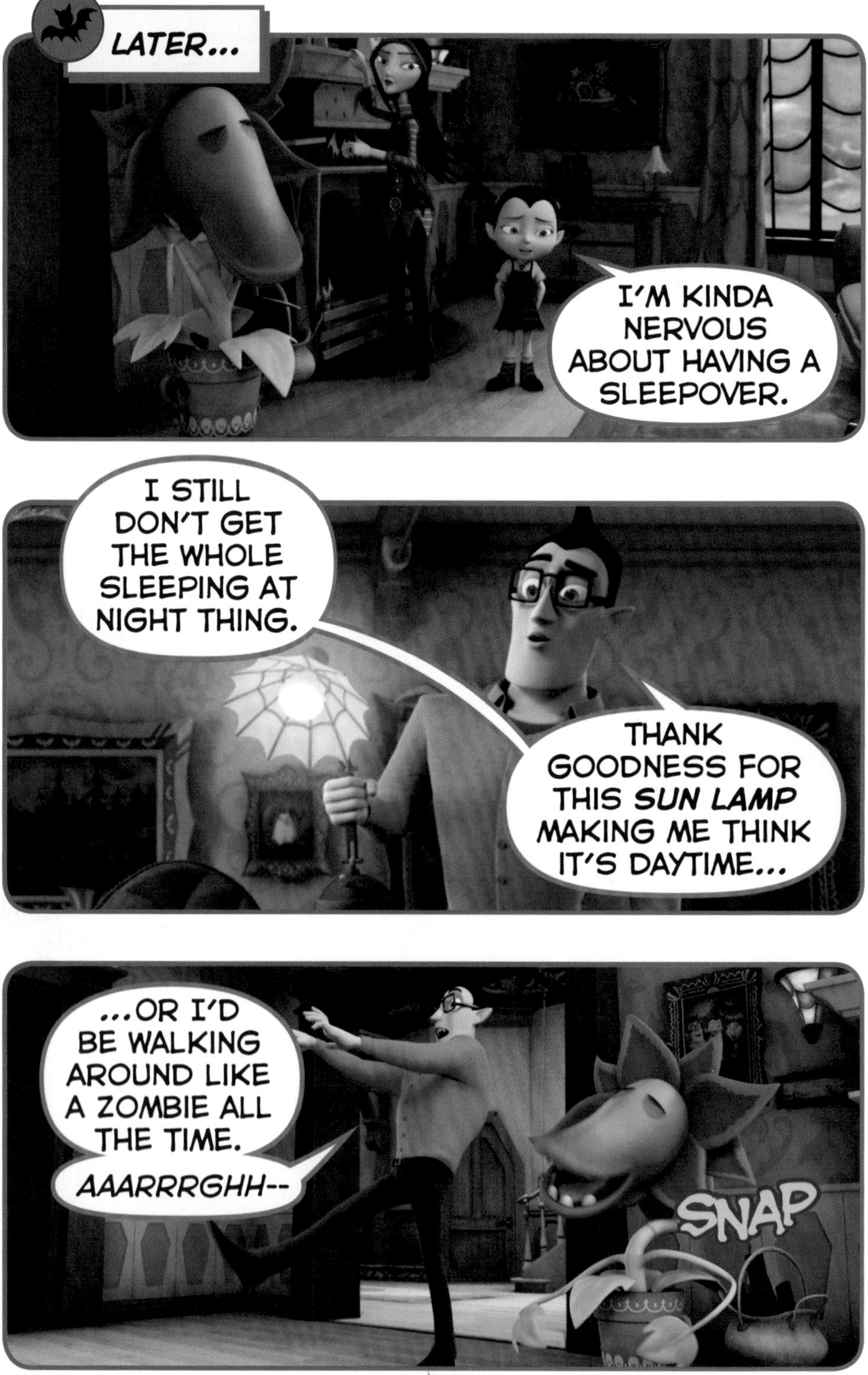
LATER...
I'M KINDA NERVOUS ABOUT HAVING A SLEEPOVER.
I STILL DON'T GET THE WHOLE SLEEPING AT NIGHT THING.
THANK GOODNESS FOR THIS *SUN LAMP* MAKING ME THINK IT'S DAYTIME...
...OR I'D BE WALKING AROUND LIKE A ZOMBIE ALL THE TIME.
AAARRRGHH--
SNAP

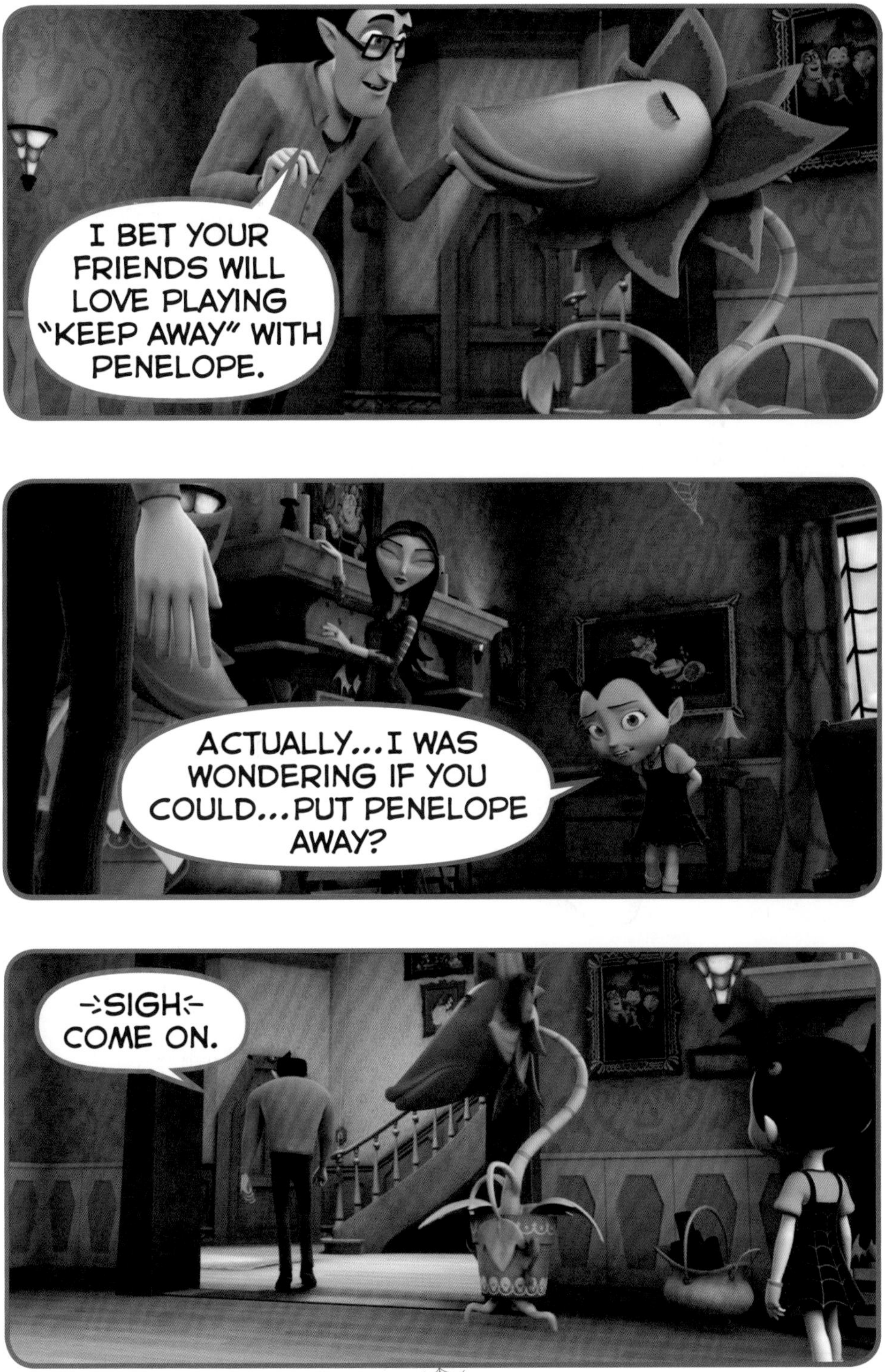
I BET YOUR FRIENDS WILL LOVE PLAYING "KEEP AWAY" WITH PENELOPE.
ACTUALLY...I WAS WONDERING IF YOU COULD...PUT PENELOPE AWAY?
SIGH
COME ON.

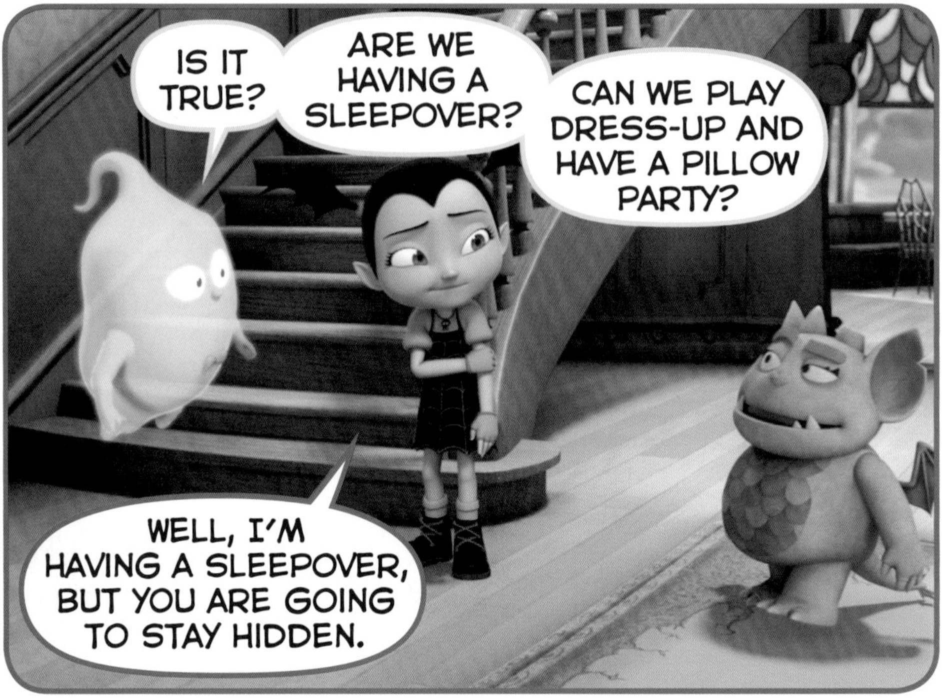
IS IT TRUE?
ARE WE HAVING A SLEEPOVER?
CAN WE PLAY DRESS-UP AND HAVE A PILLOW PARTY?
WELL, I'M HAVING A SLEEPOVER, BUT YOU ARE GOING TO STAY HIDDEN.

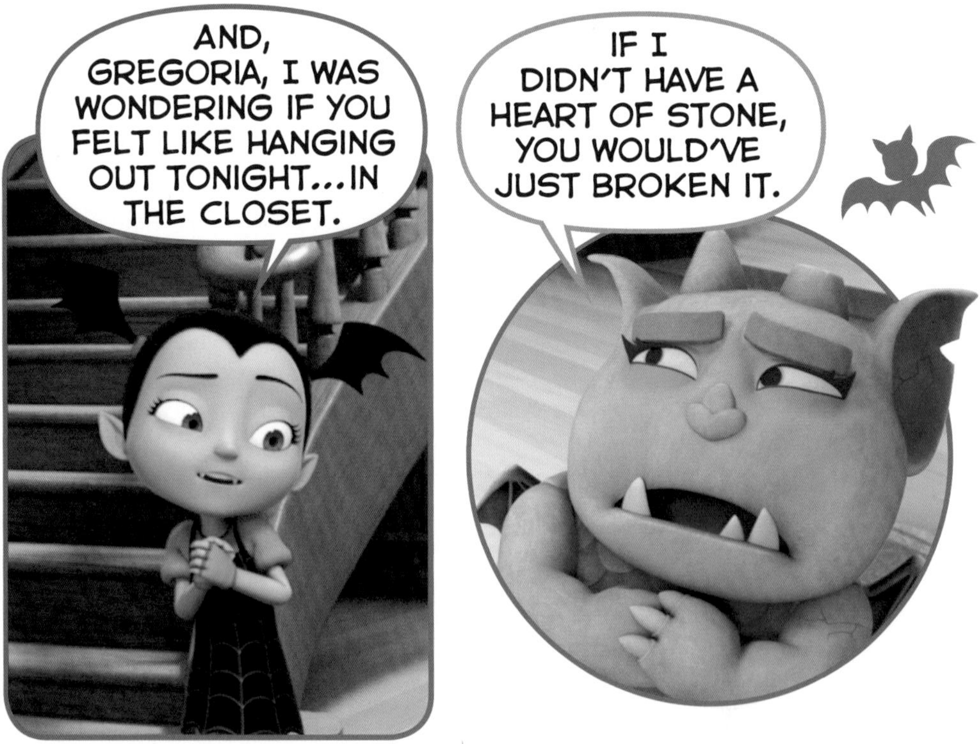
AND, GREGORIA, I WAS WONDERING IF YOU FELT LIKE HANGING OUT TONIGHT...IN THE CLOSET.
IF I DIDN'T HAVE A HEART OF STONE, YOU WOULD'VE JUST BROKEN IT.

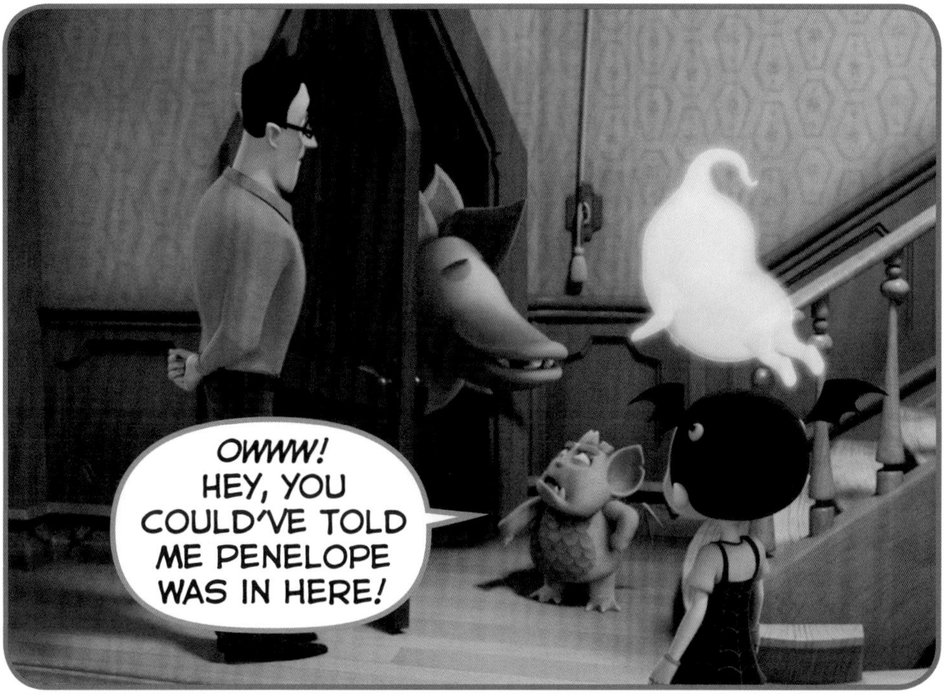
OWWW! HEY, YOU COULD'VE TOLD ME PENELOPE WAS IN HERE!

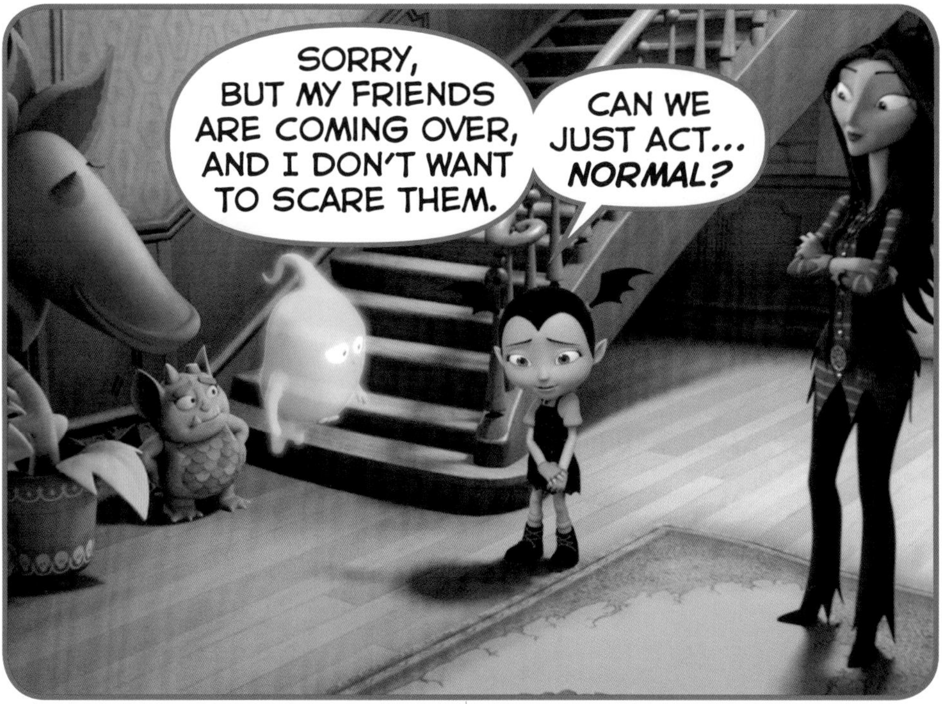
SORRY, BUT MY FRIENDS ARE COMING OVER, AND I DON'T WANT TO SCARE THEM.
CAN WE JUST ACT... NORMAL?

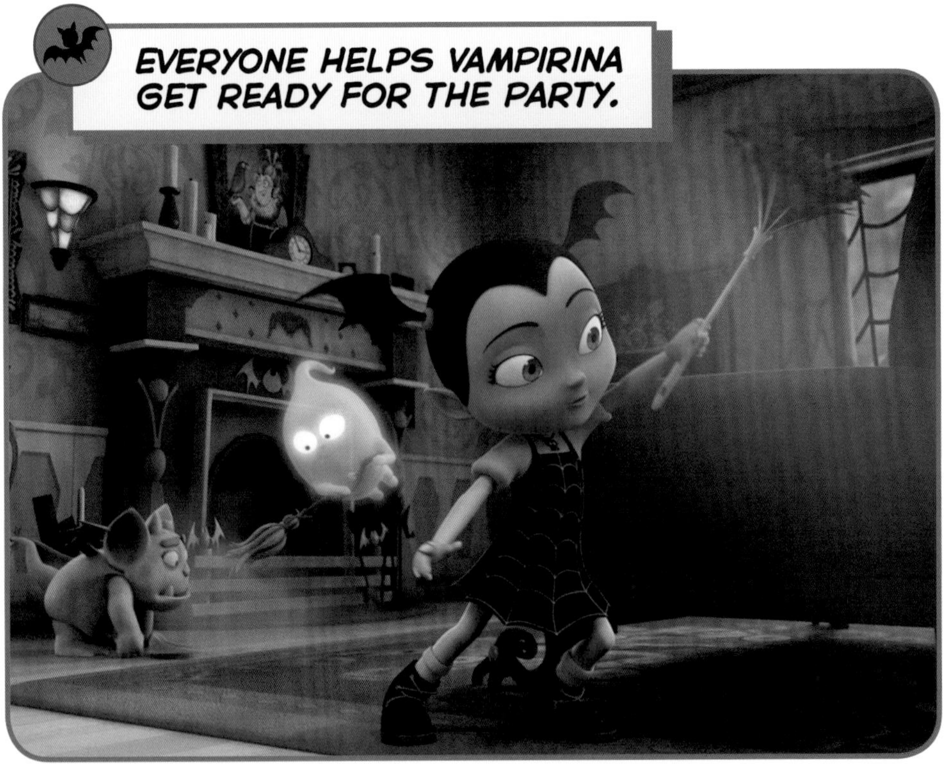
EVERYONE HELPS VAMPIRINA
GET READY FOR THE PARTY.

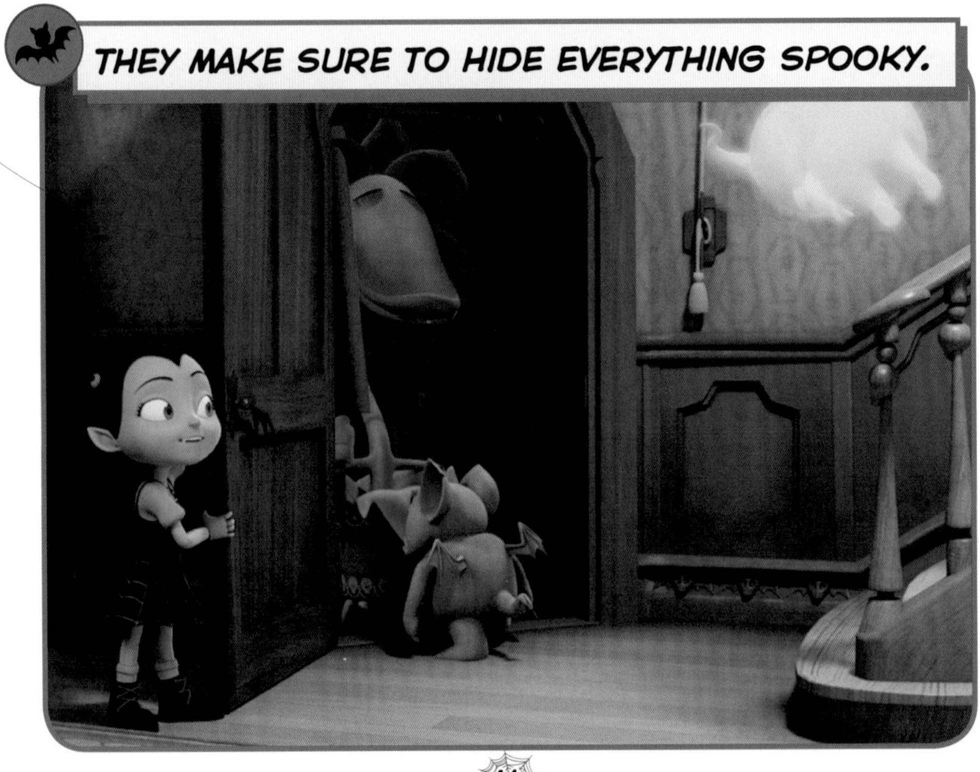
THEY MAKE SURE TO HIDE EVERYTHING SPOOKY.

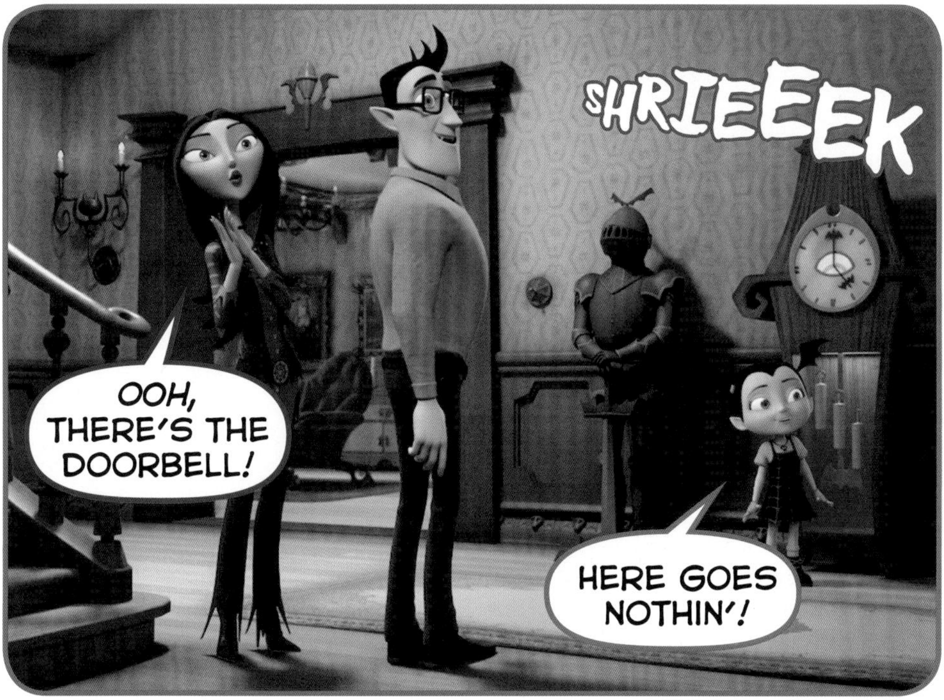
SHRIEEEK
OOH, THERE'S THE DOORBELL!
HERE GOES NOTHIN'!

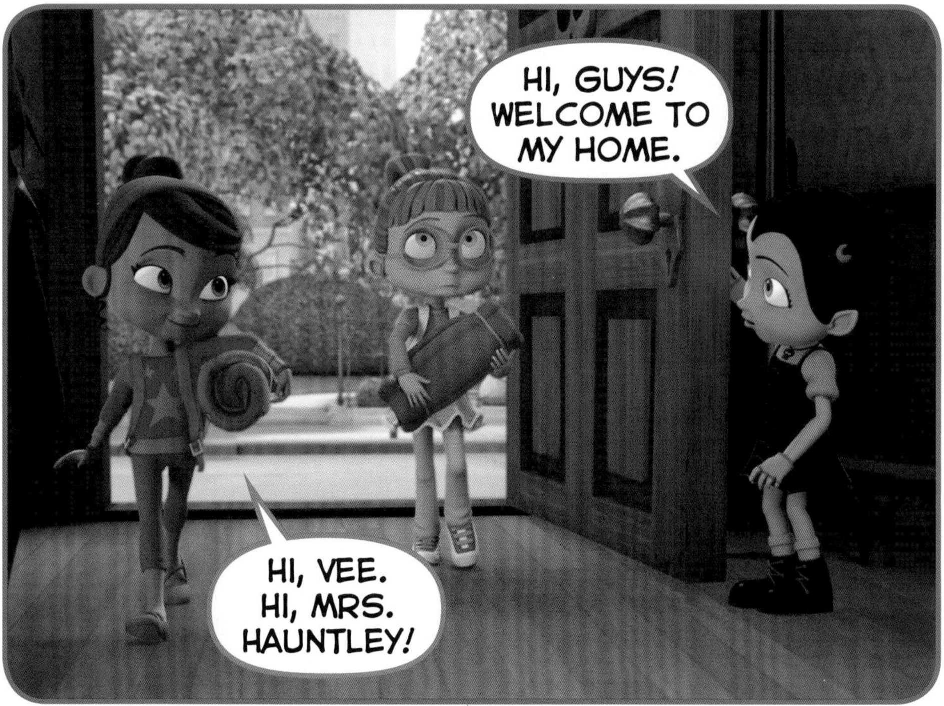
HI, GUYS! WELCOME TO MY HOME.
HI, VEE. HI, MRS. HAUNTLEY!

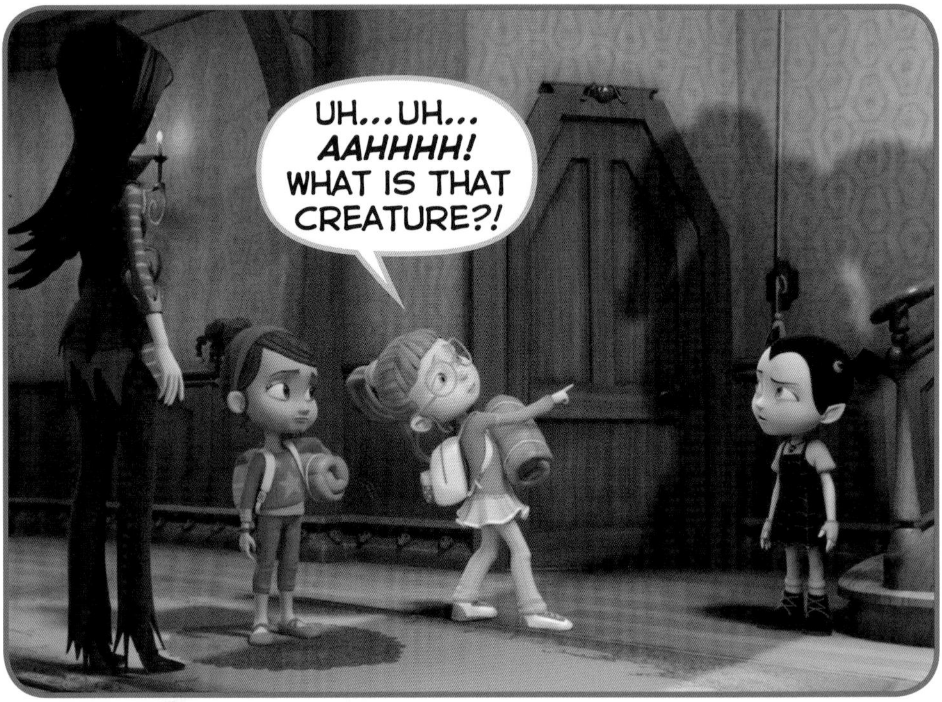
UH...UH... AAHHHH! WHAT IS THAT CREATURE?!

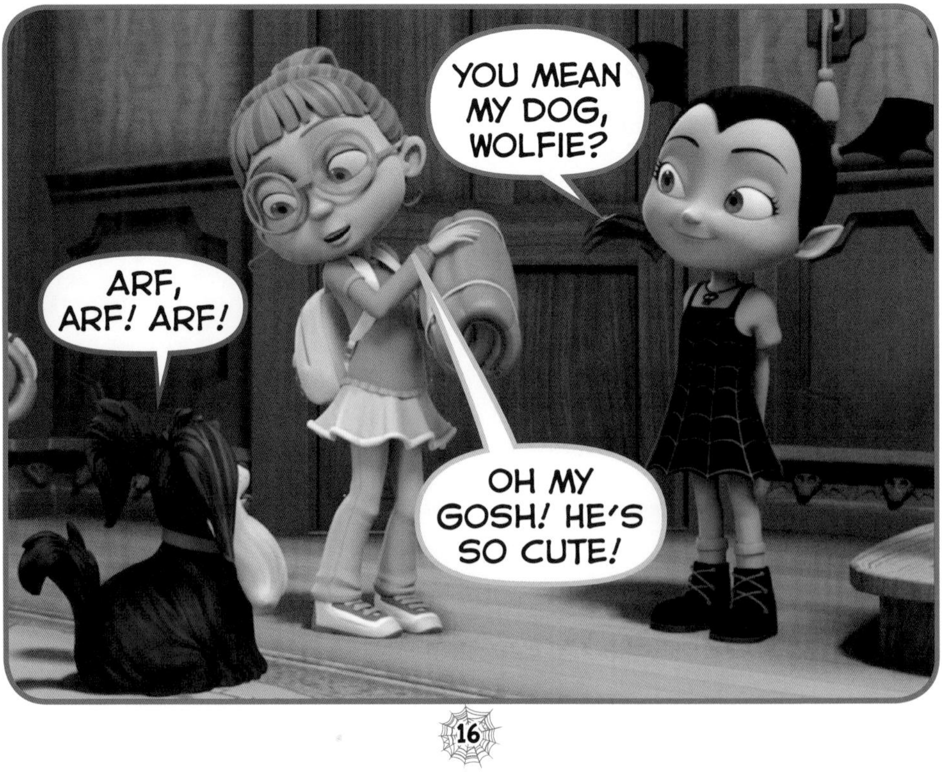
YOU MEAN MY DOG, WOLFIE?
ARF, ARF! ARF!
OH MY GOSH! HE'S SO CUTE!

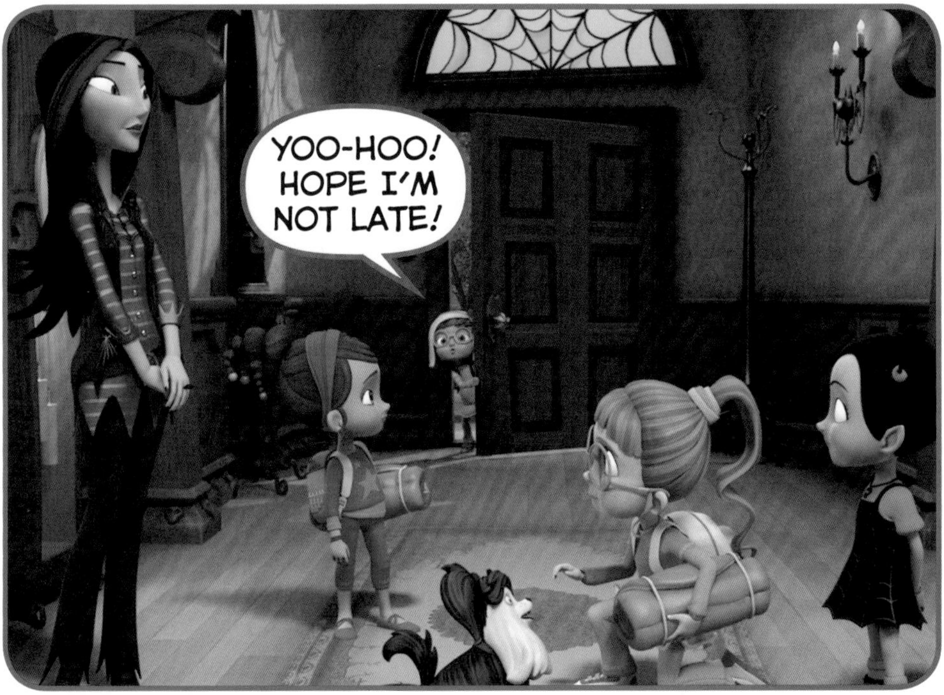
YOO-HOO! HOPE I'M NOT LATE!

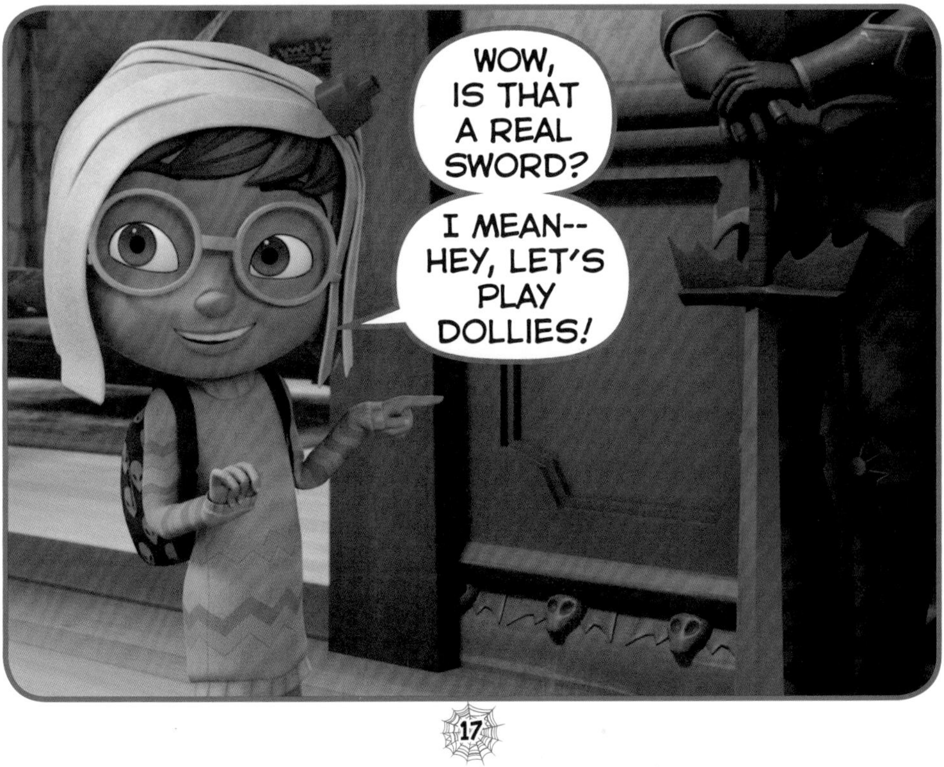
WOW, IS THAT A REAL SWORD?
I MEAN-- HEY, LET'S PLAY DOLLIES!

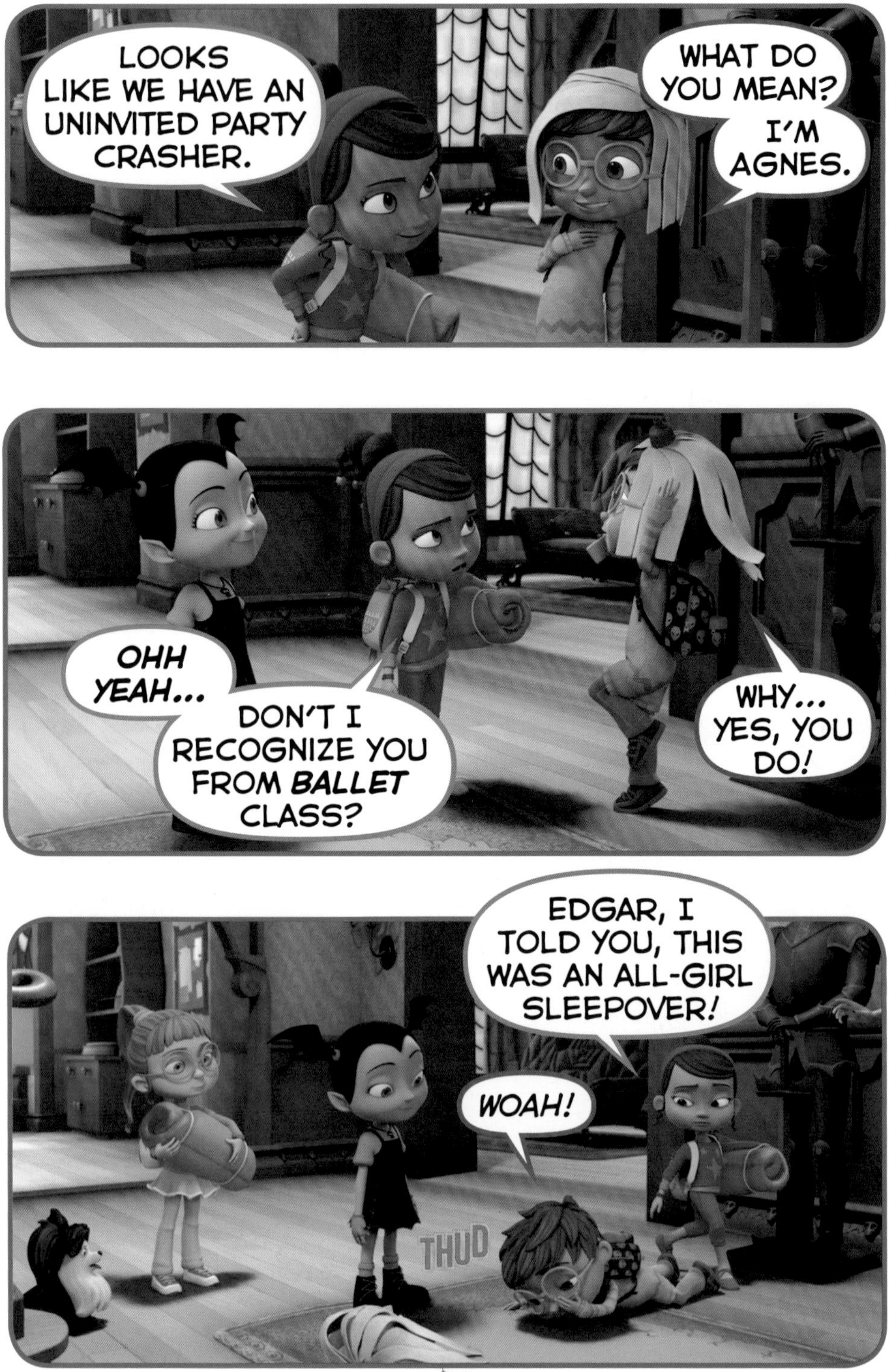
LOOKS LIKE WE HAVE AN UNINVITED PARTY CRASHER.
WHAT DO YOU MEAN?
I'M AGNES.
OHH YEAH...
DON'T I RECOGNIZE YOU FROM BALLET CLASS?
WHY... YES, YOU DO!
EDGAR, I TOLD YOU, THIS WAS AN ALL-GIRL SLEEPOVER!
WOAH!
THUD

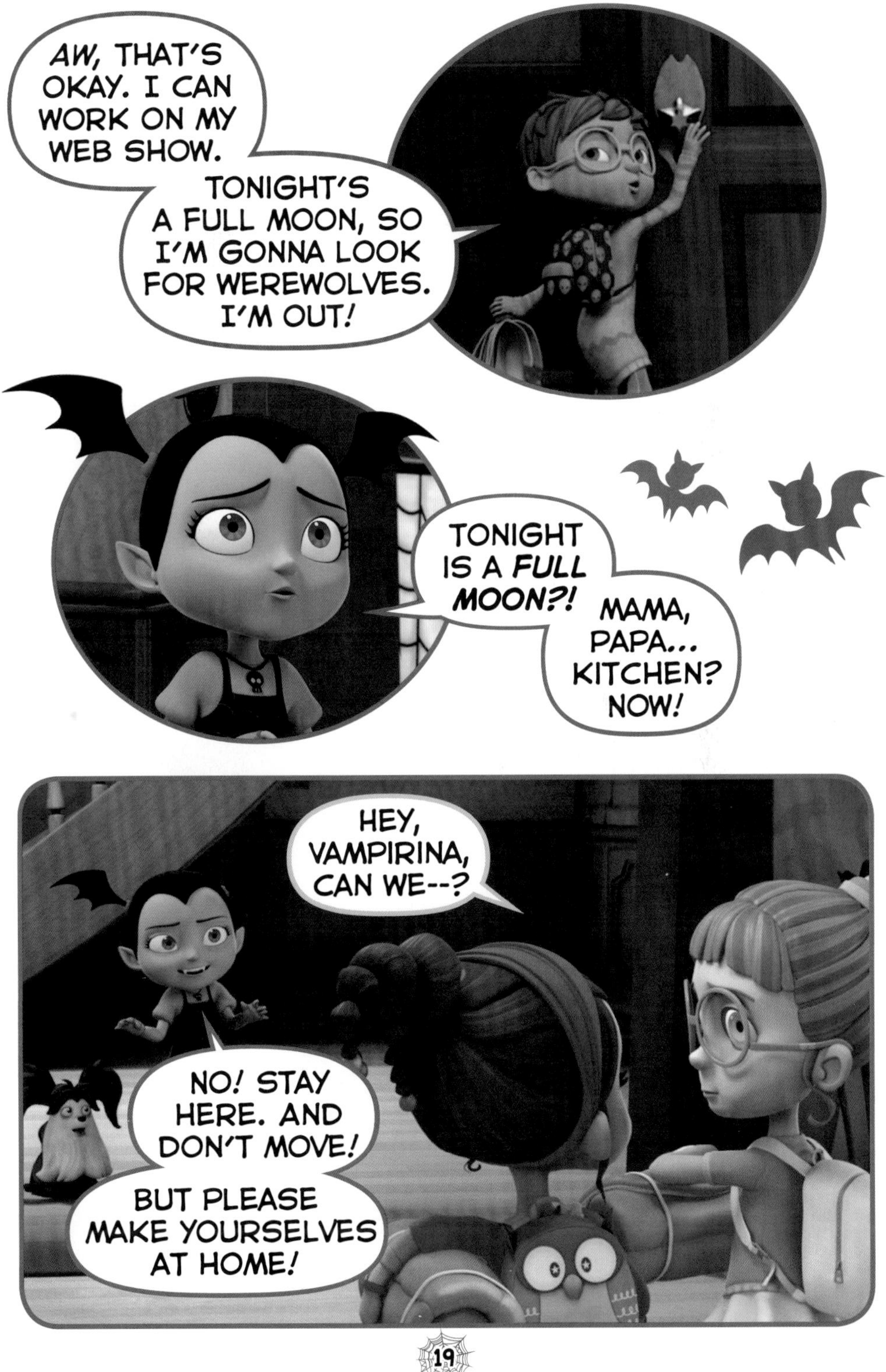
AW, THAT'S OKAY. I CAN WORK ON MY WEB SHOW.
TONIGHT'S A FULL MOON, SO I'M GONNA LOOK FOR WEREWOLVES. I'M OUT!
TONIGHT IS A *FULL MOON?!*
MAMA, PAPA... KITCHEN? NOW!
HEY, VAMPIRINA, CAN WE--?
NO! STAY HERE. AND DON'T MOVE!
BUT PLEASE MAKE YOURSELVES AT HOME!

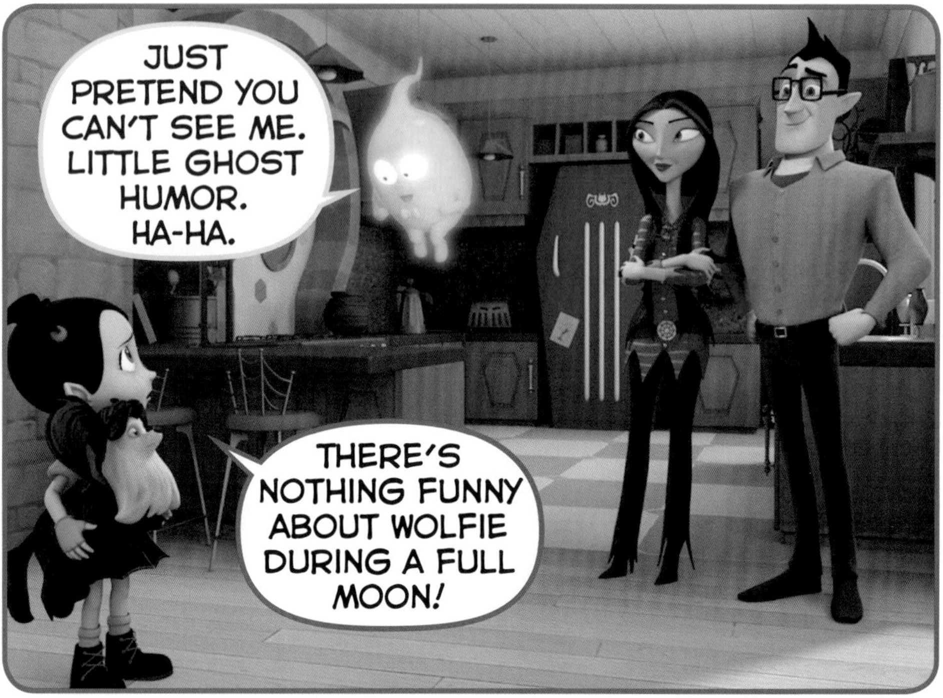
JUST PRETEND YOU CAN'T SEE ME. LITTLE GHOST HUMOR. HA-HA.
THERE'S NOTHING FUNNY ABOUT WOLFIE DURING A FULL MOON!

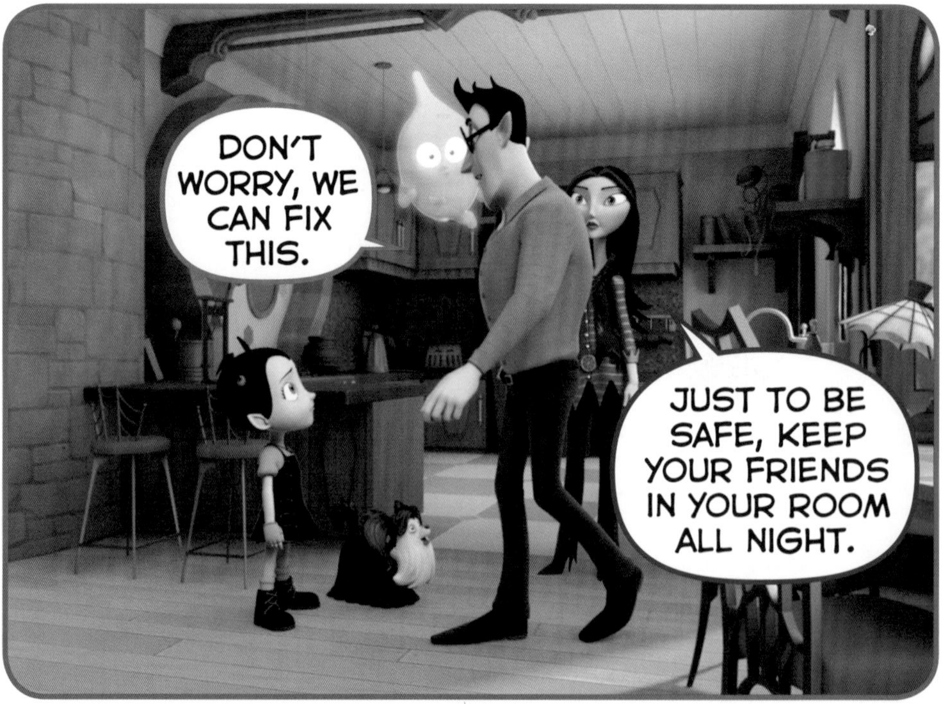
DON'T WORRY, WE CAN FIX THIS.
JUST TO BE SAFE, KEEP YOUR FRIENDS IN YOUR ROOM ALL NIGHT.

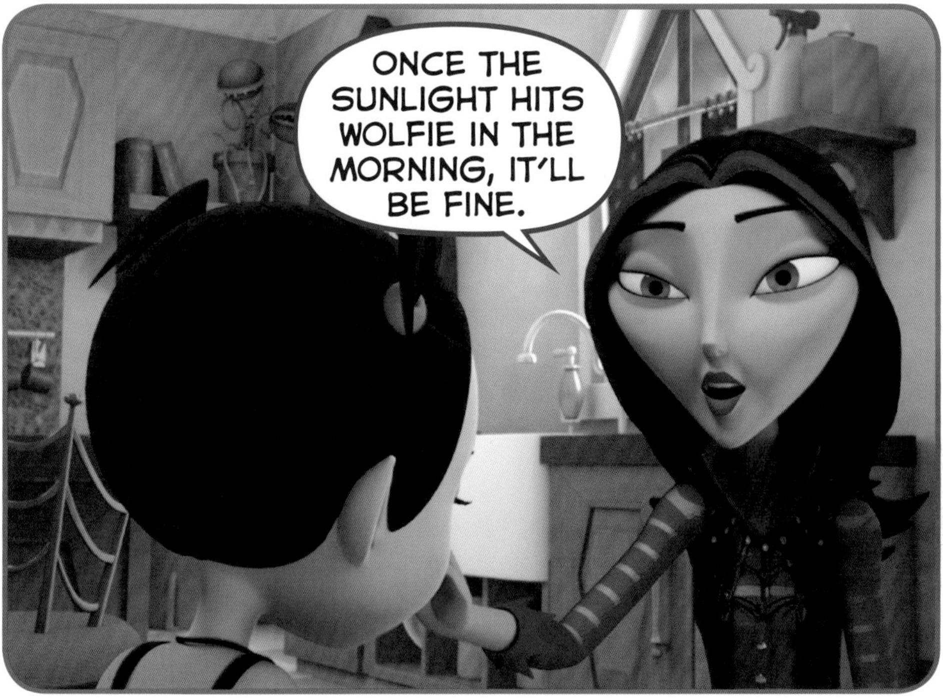
ONCE THE SUNLIGHT HITS WOLFIE IN THE MORNING, IT'LL BE FINE.

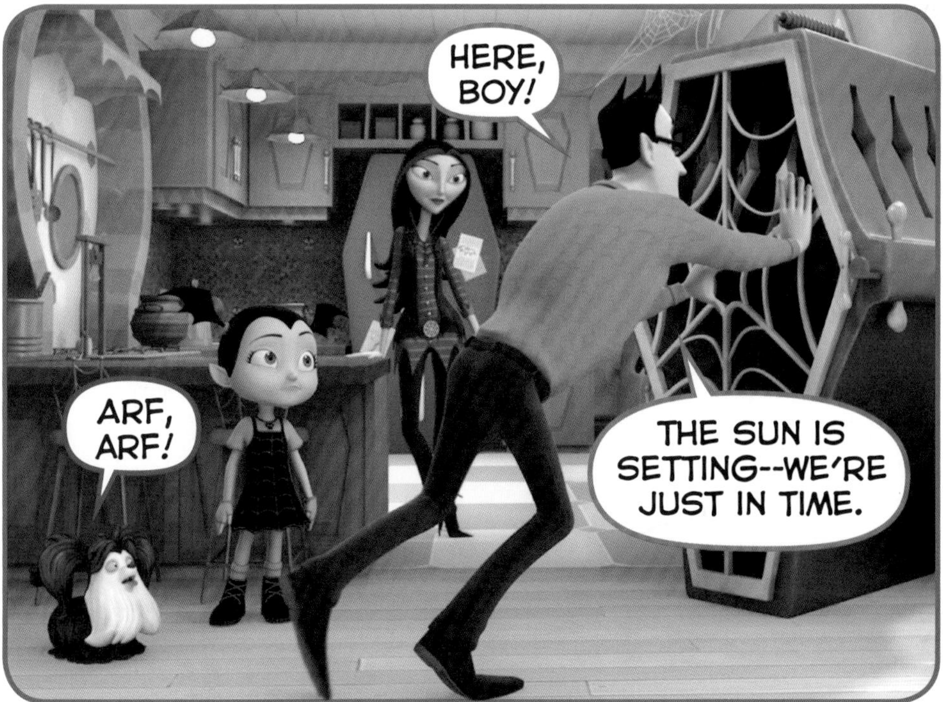
HERE, BOY!
ARF, ARF!
THE SUN IS SETTING--WE'RE JUST IN TIME.

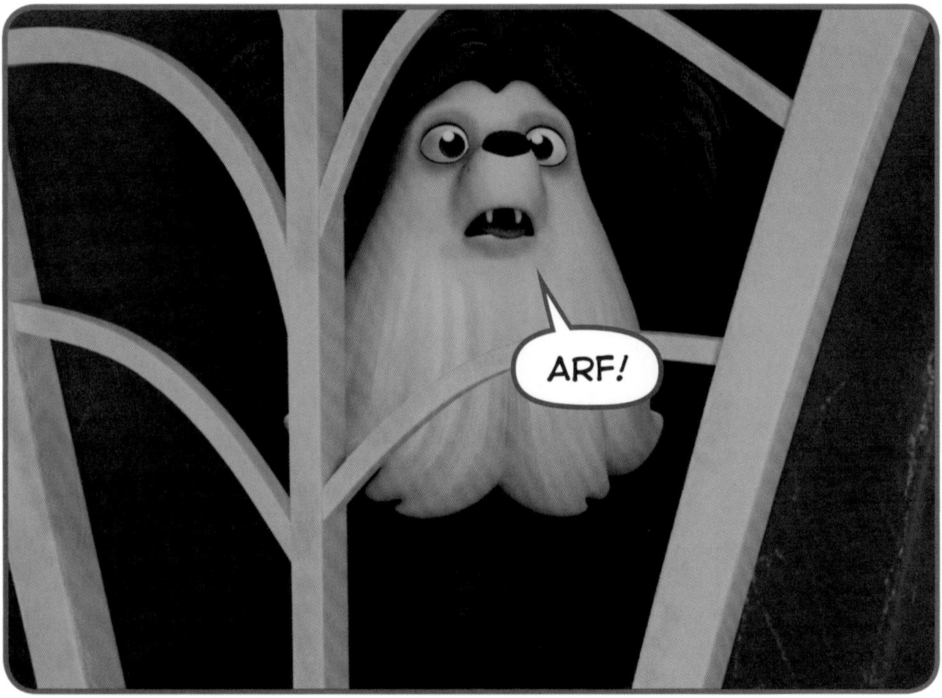
ARF!

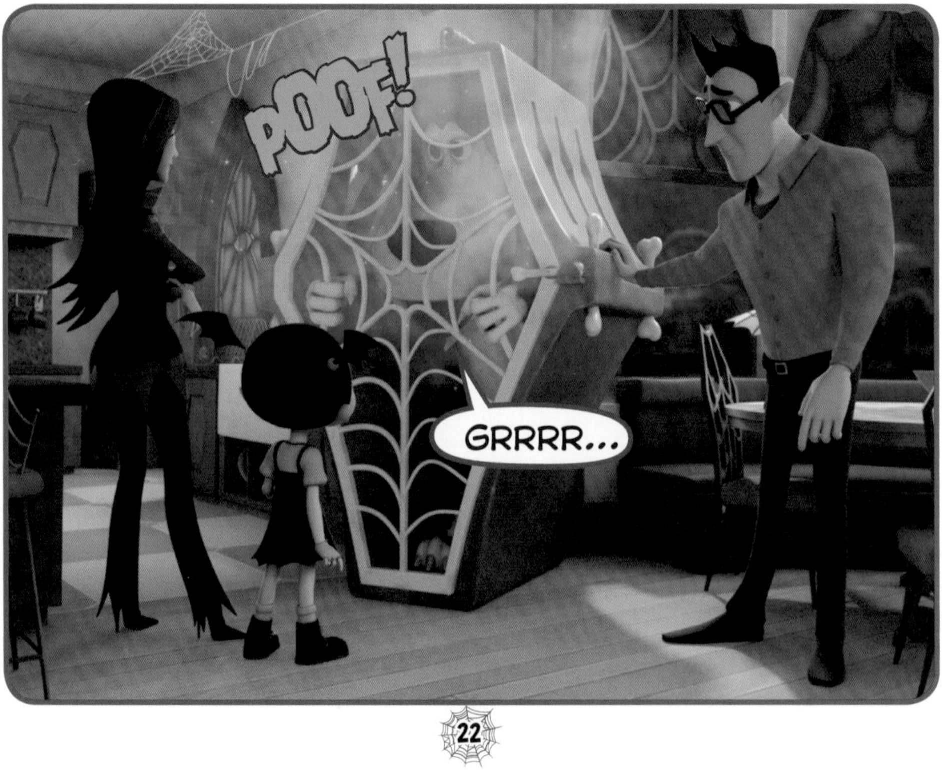
POOF!
GRRRR...

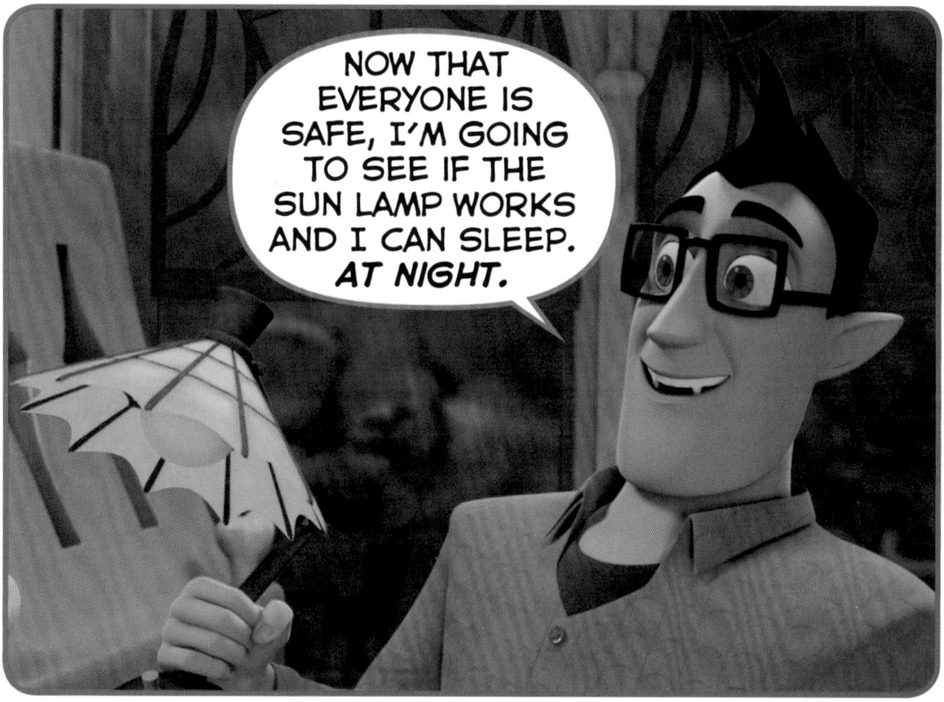
NOW THAT EVERYONE IS SAFE, I'M GOING TO SEE IF THE SUN LAMP WORKS AND I CAN SLEEP. *AT NIGHT.*

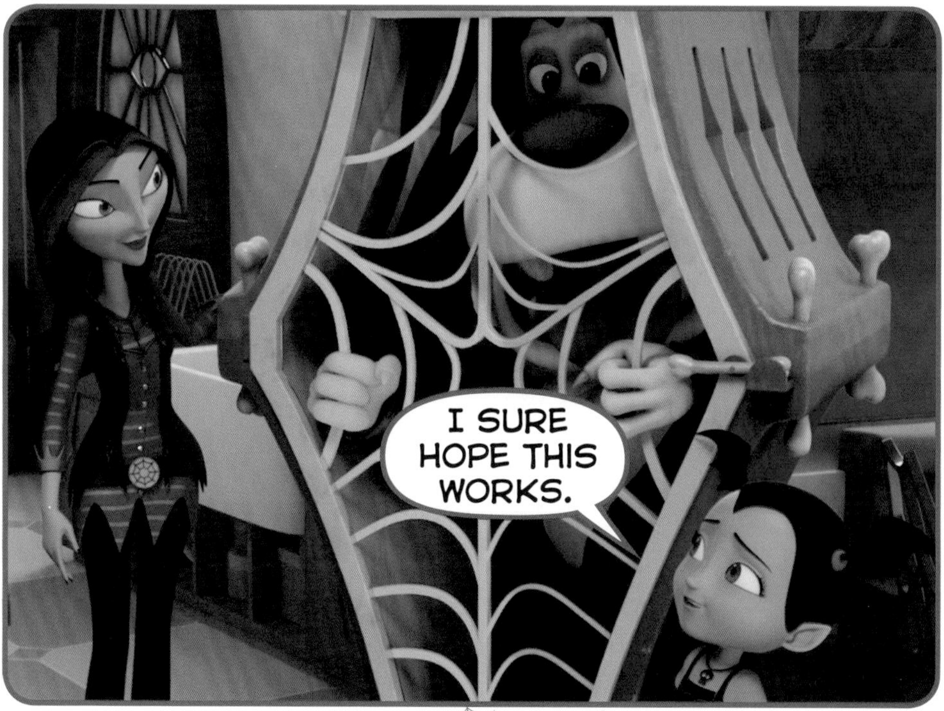
I SURE HOPE THIS WORKS.

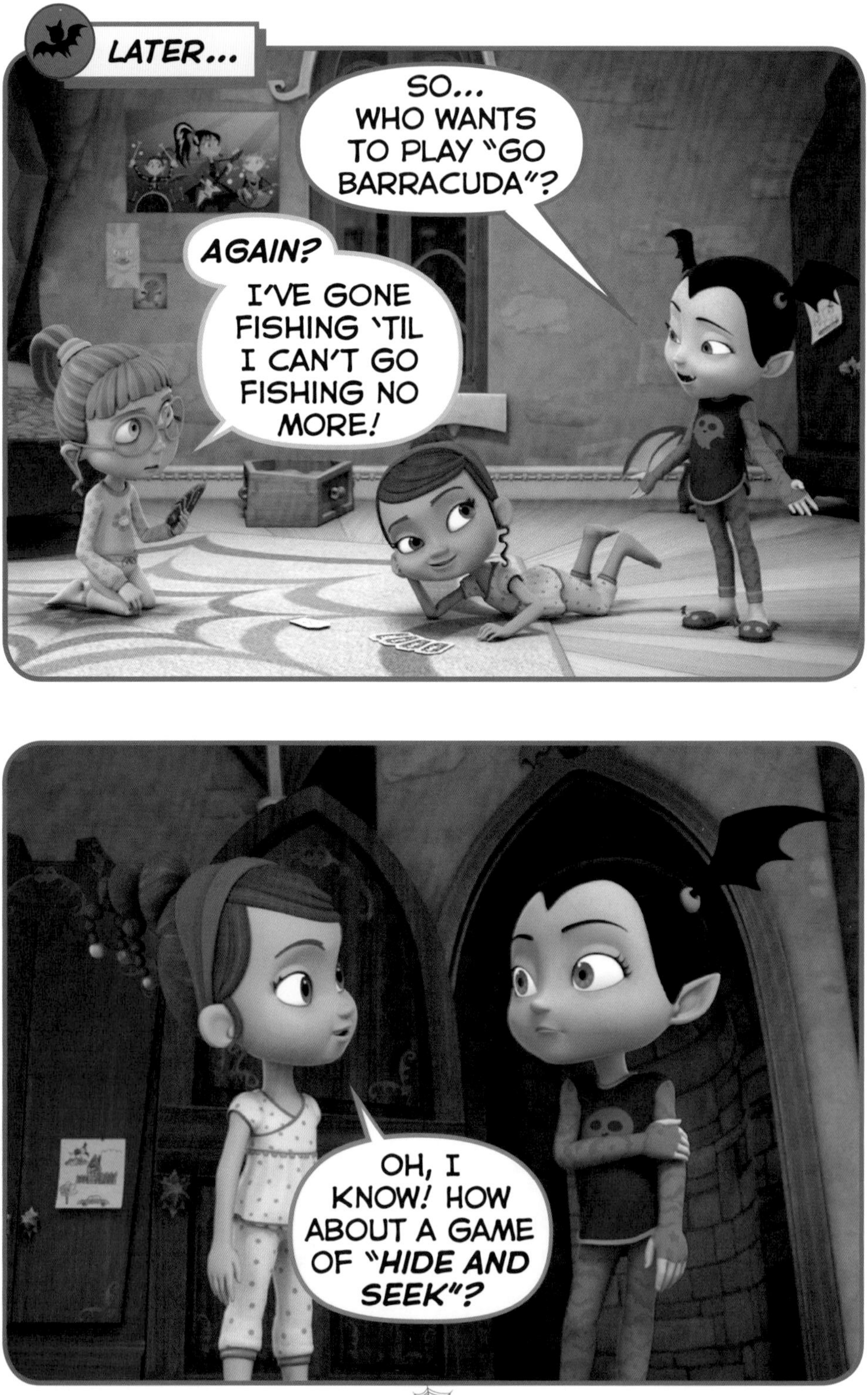
LATER...
SO... WHO WANTS TO PLAY "GO BARRACUDA"?
AGAIN?
I'VE GONE FISHING 'TIL I CAN'T GO FISHING NO MORE!
OH, I KNOW! HOW ABOUT A GAME OF "HIDE AND SEEK"?

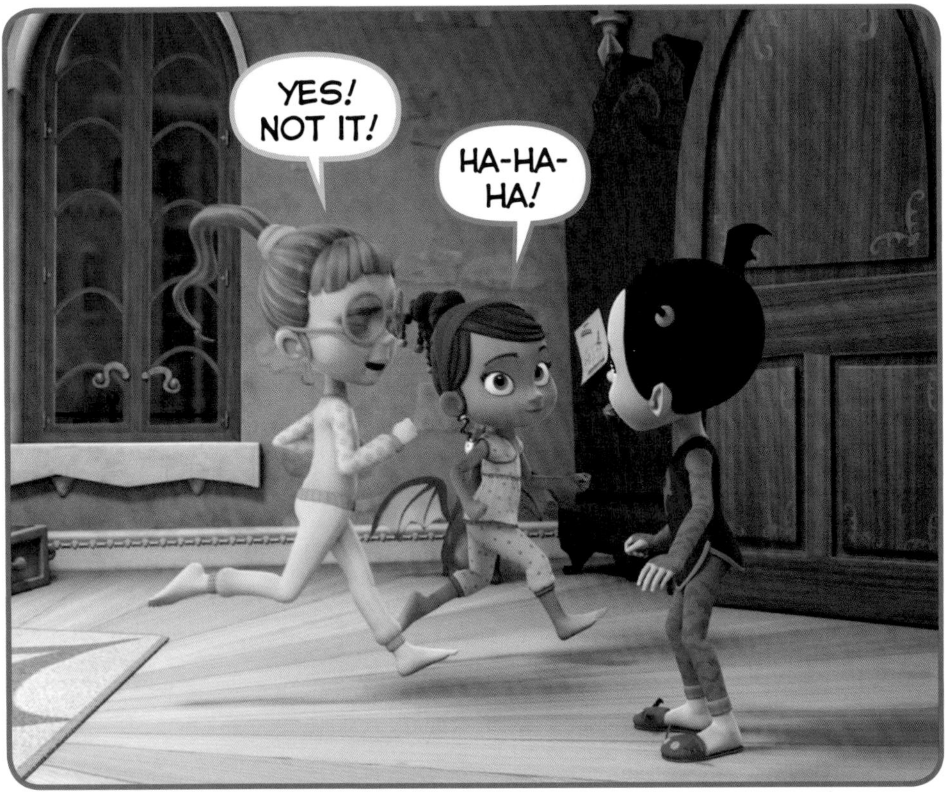
YES! NOT IT!
HA-HA-HA!

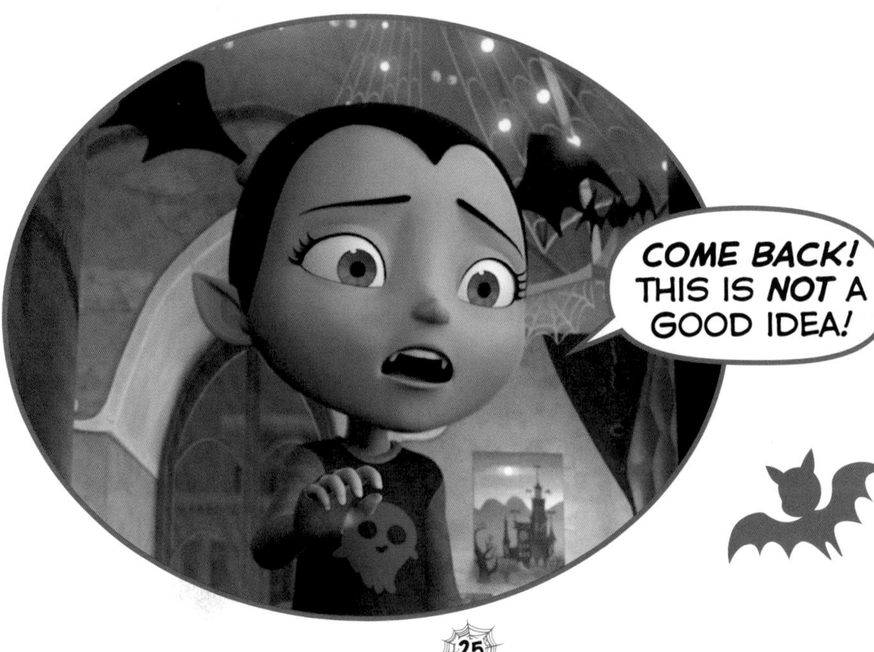
COME BACK! THIS IS NOT A GOOD IDEA!

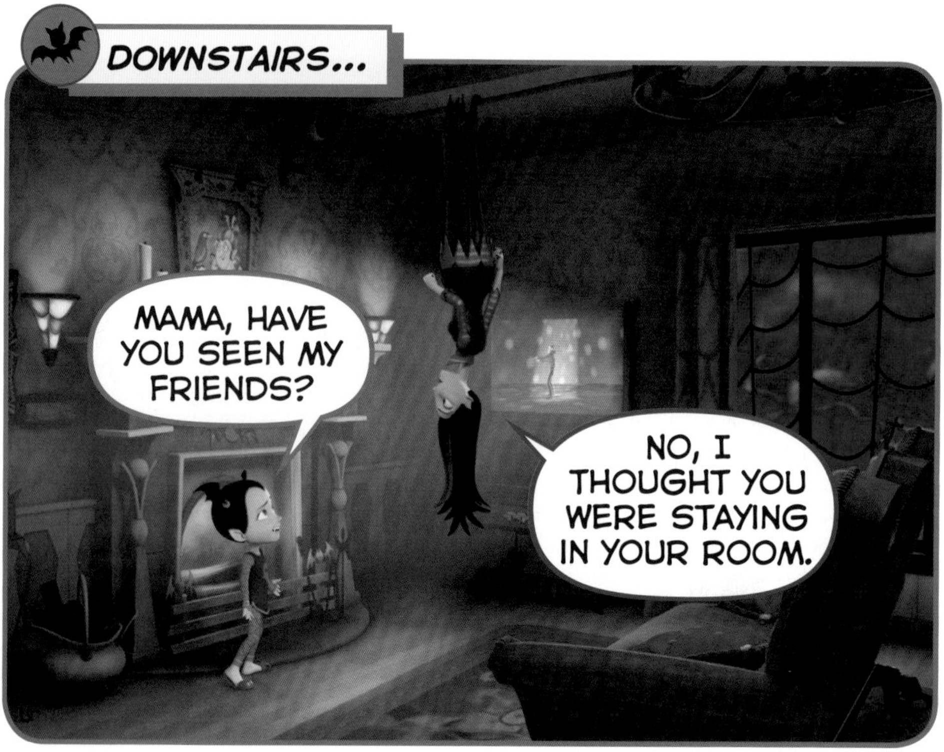
DOWNSTAIRS...
MAMA, HAVE YOU SEEN MY FRIENDS?
NO, I THOUGHT YOU WERE STAYING IN YOUR ROOM.

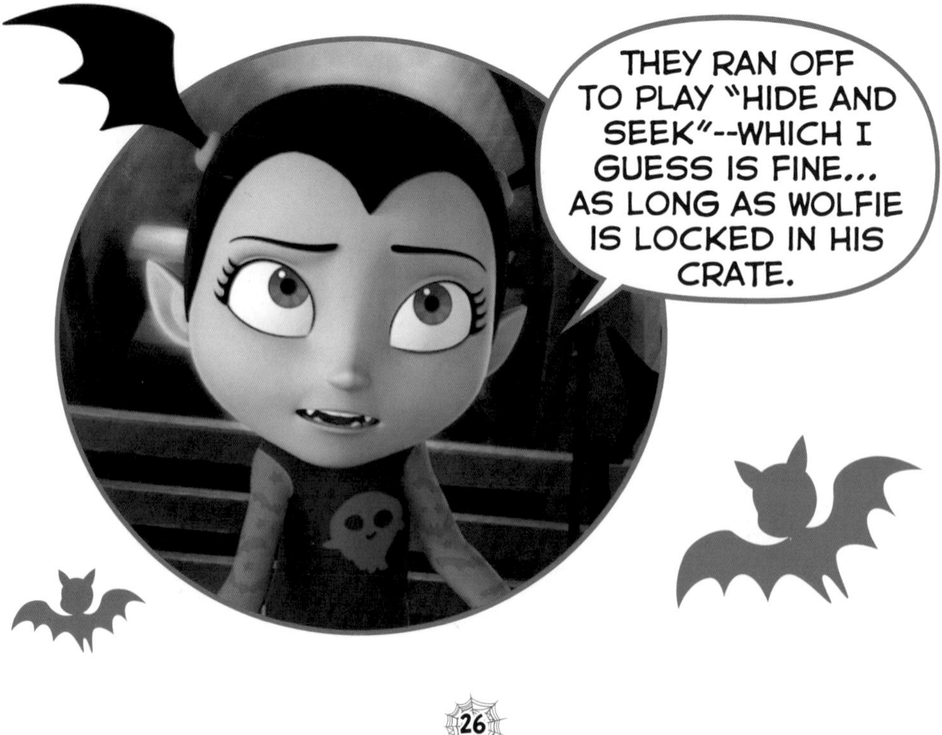
THEY RAN OFF TO PLAY "HIDE AND SEEK"--WHICH I GUESS IS FINE... AS LONG AS WOLFIE IS LOCKED IN HIS CRATE.

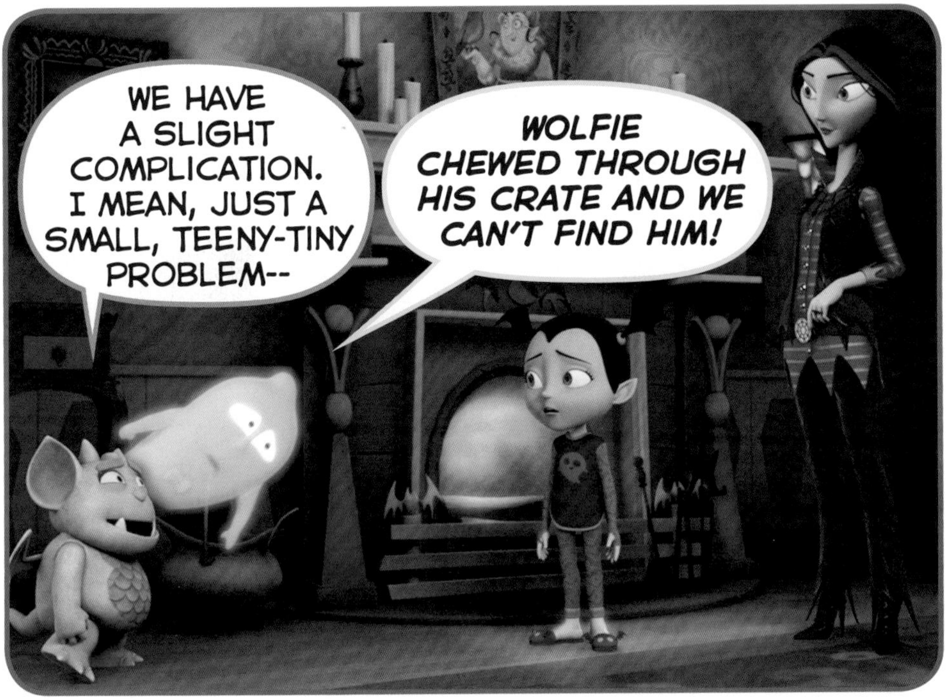
WE HAVE A SLIGHT COMPLICATION. I MEAN, JUST A SMALL, TEENY-TINY PROBLEM--
WOLFIE CHEWED THROUGH HIS CRATE AND WE CAN'T FIND HIM!

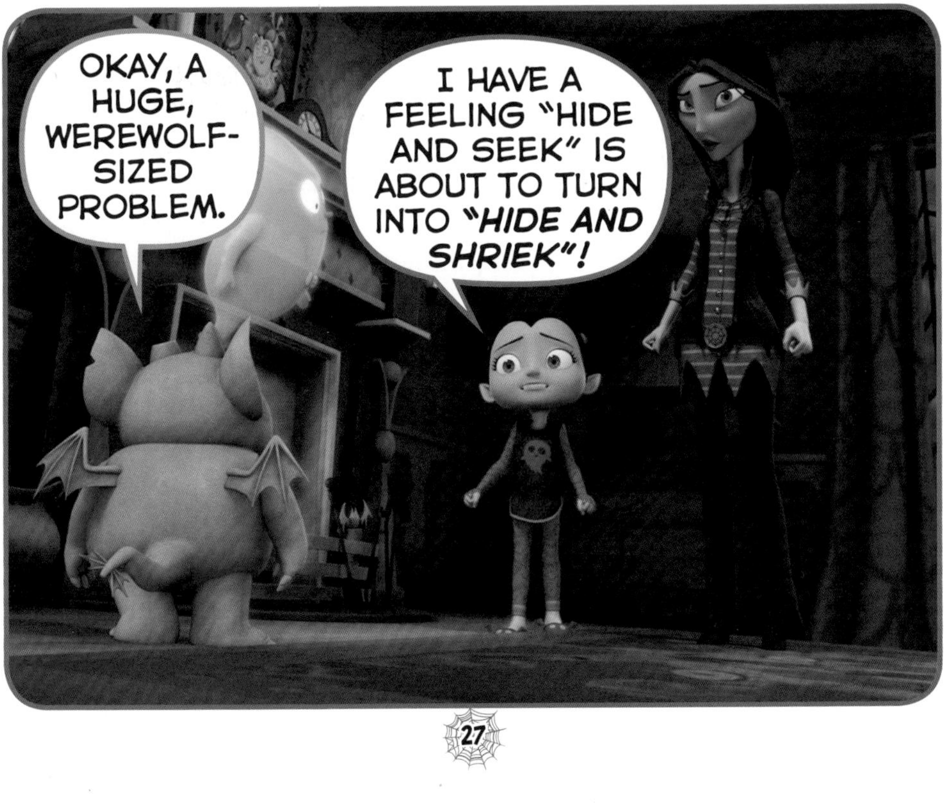
OKAY, A HUGE, WEREWOLF-SIZED PROBLEM.
I HAVE A FEELING "HIDE AND SEEK" IS ABOUT TO TURN INTO "HIDE AND SHRIEK"!

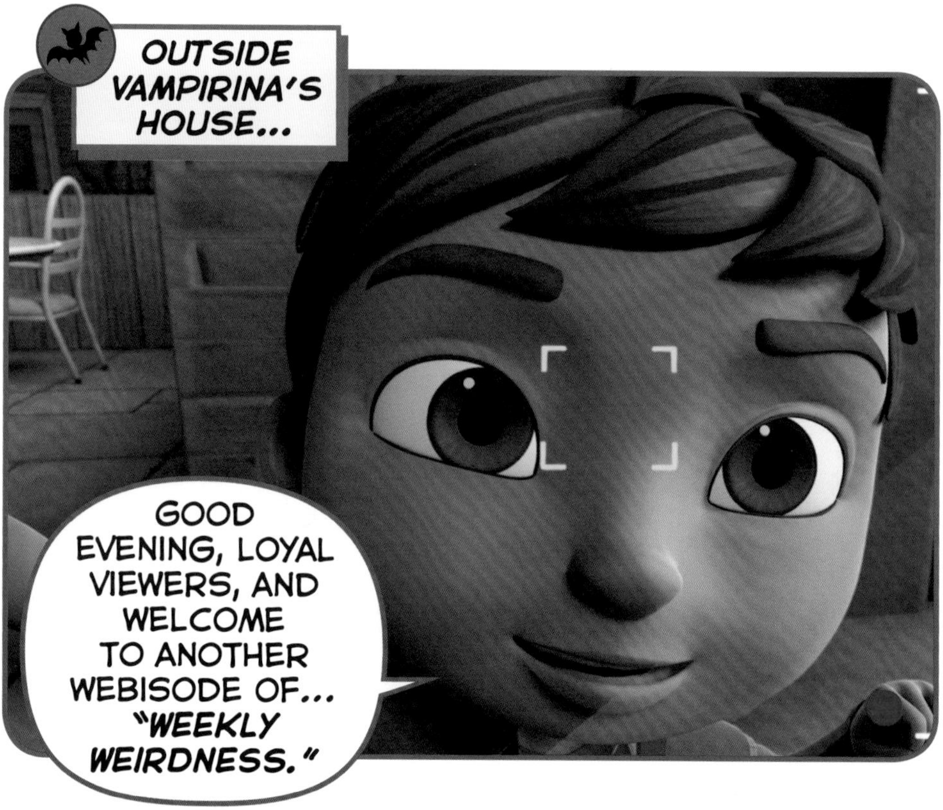
OUTSIDE VAMPIRINA'S HOUSE...
GOOD EVENING, LOYAL VIEWERS, AND WELCOME TO ANOTHER WEBISODE OF... "WEEKLY WEIRDNESS."

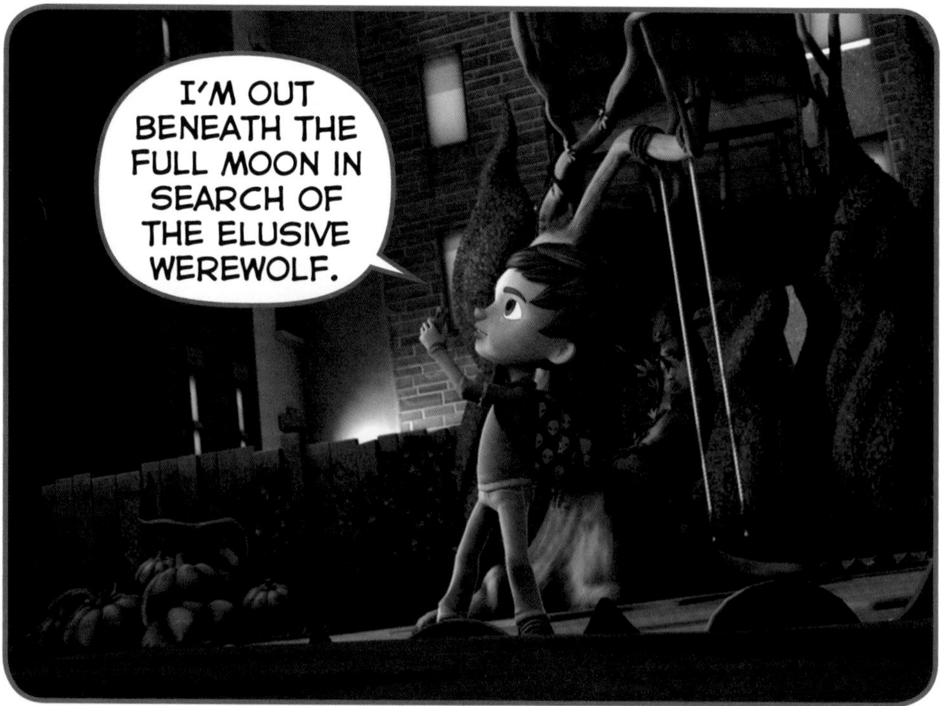
I'M OUT BENEATH THE FULL MOON IN SEARCH OF THE ELUSIVE WEREWOLF.

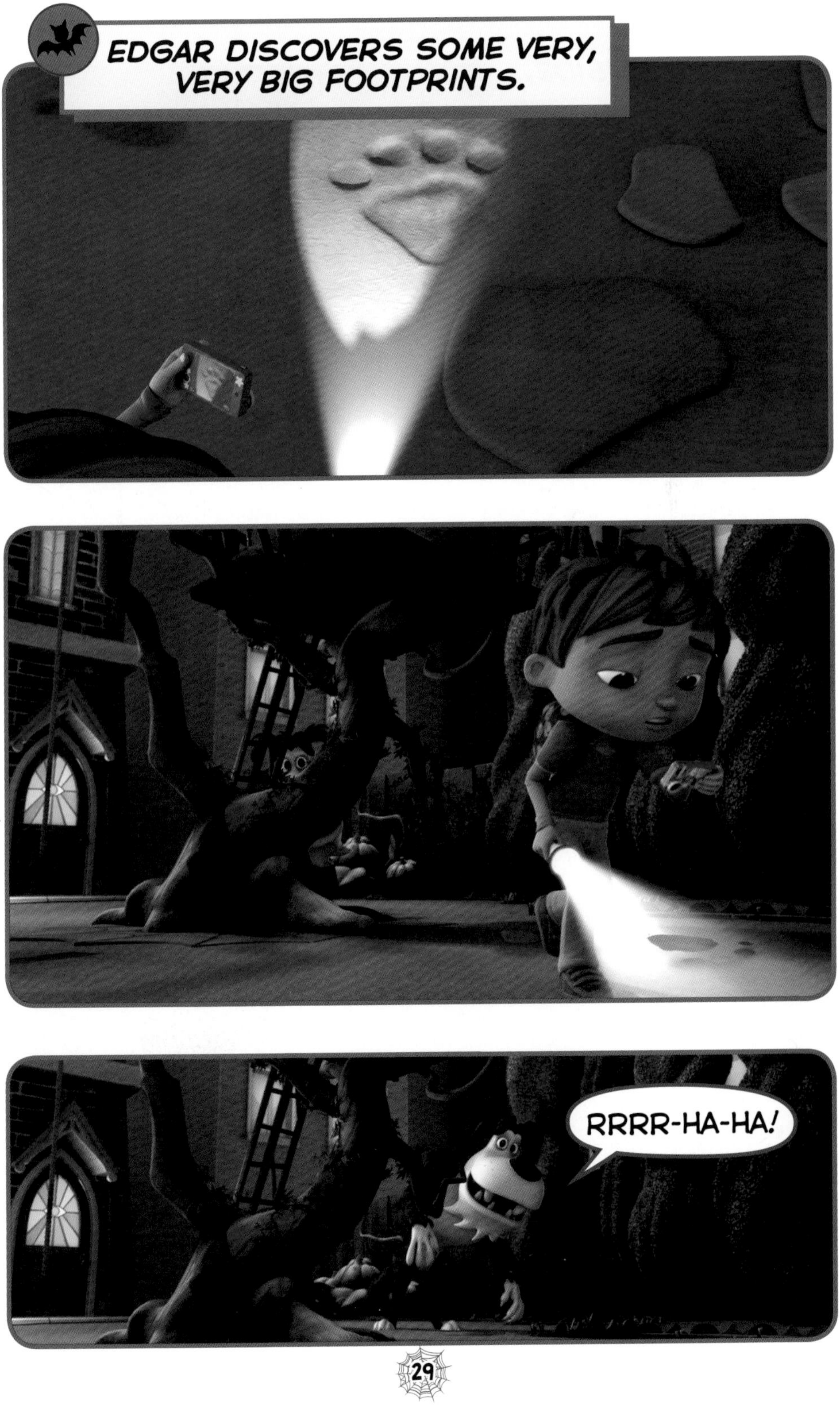
EDGAR DISCOVERS SOME VERY, VERY BIG FOOTPRINTS.
RRRR-HA-HA!

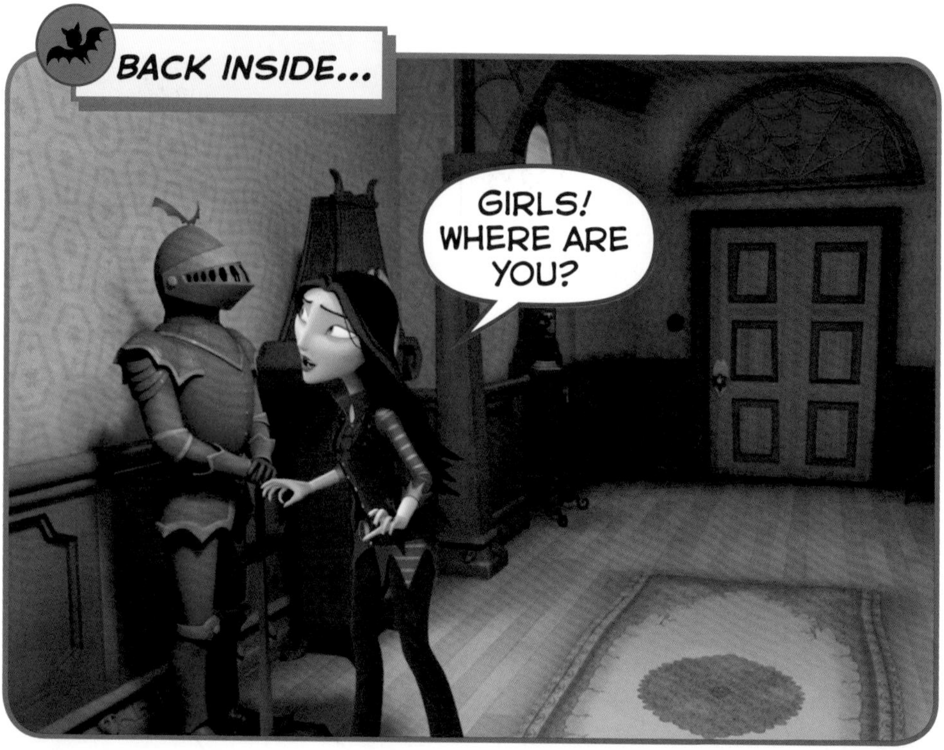
BACK INSIDE...
GIRLS! WHERE ARE YOU?

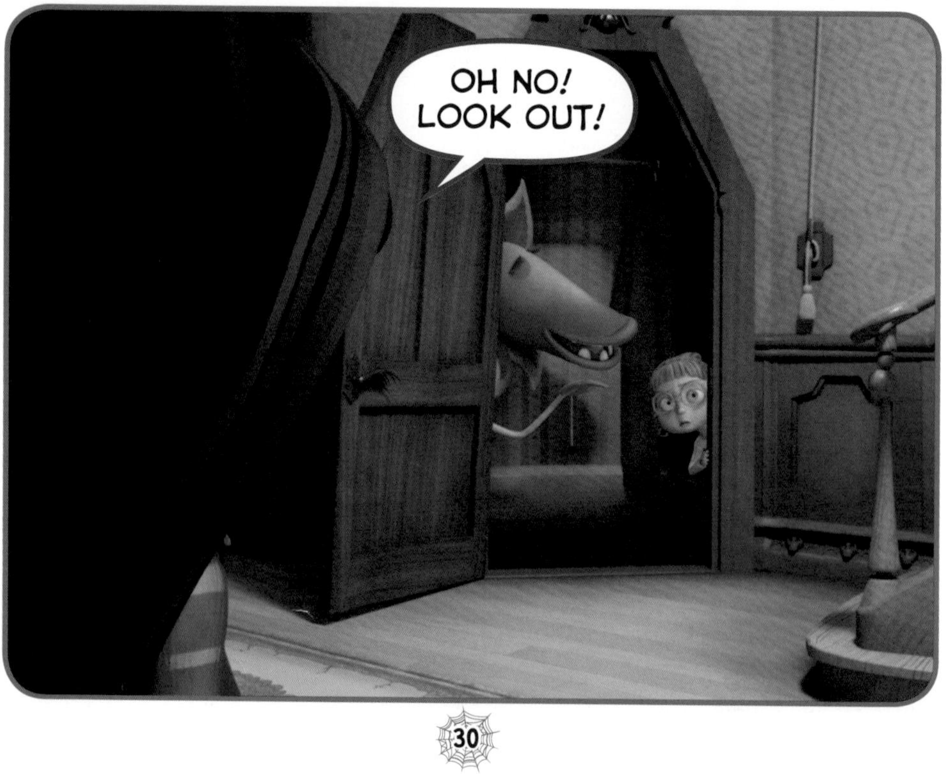
OH NO! LOOK OUT!

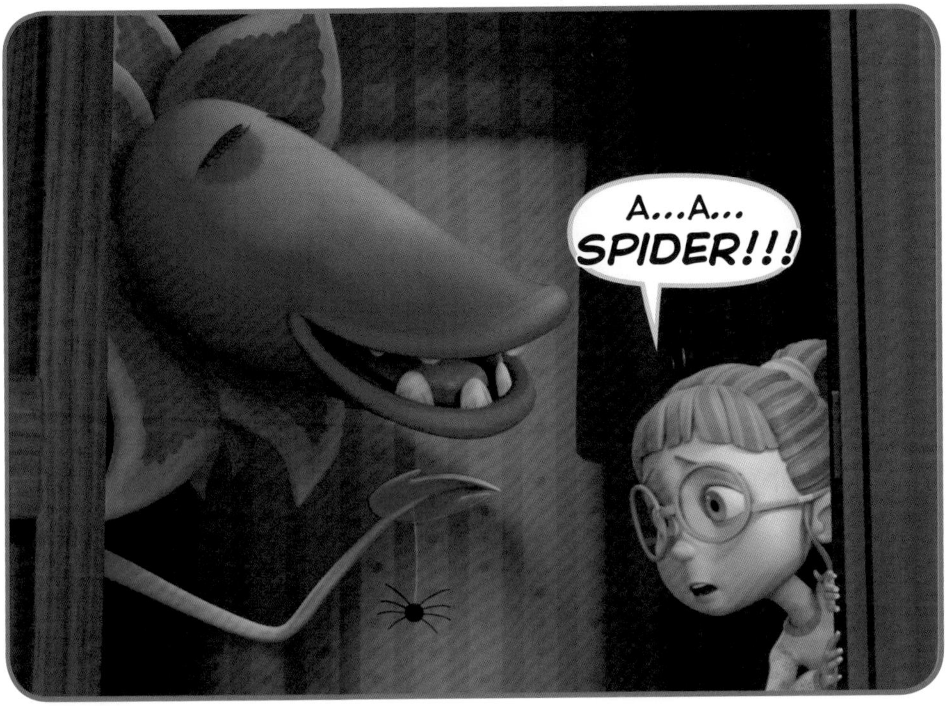
A...A...
SPIDER!!!

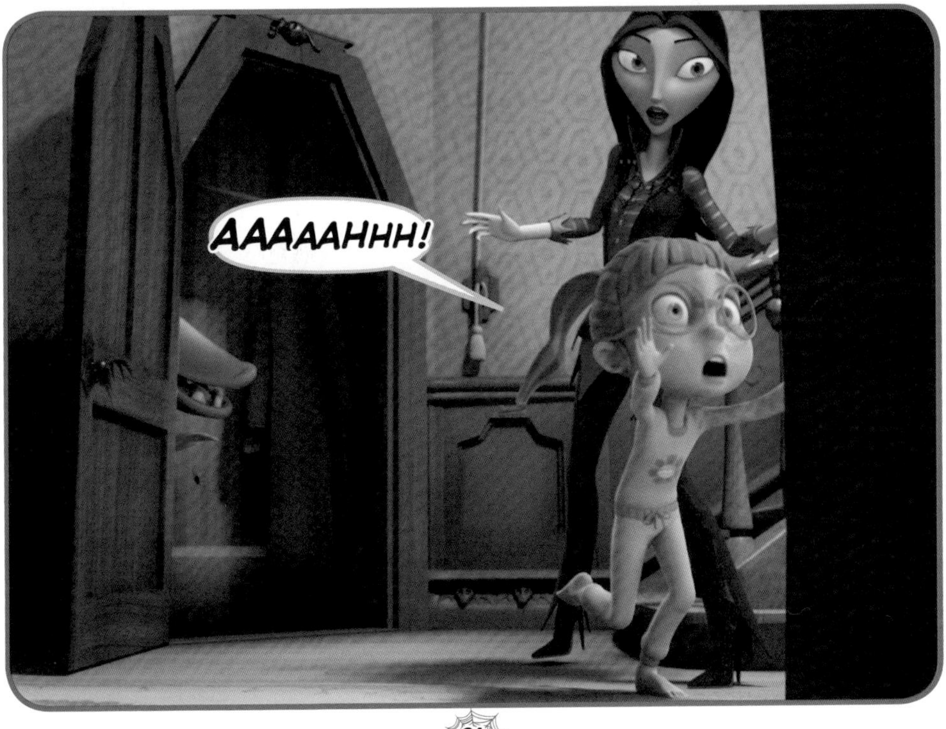
AAAAAHHH!

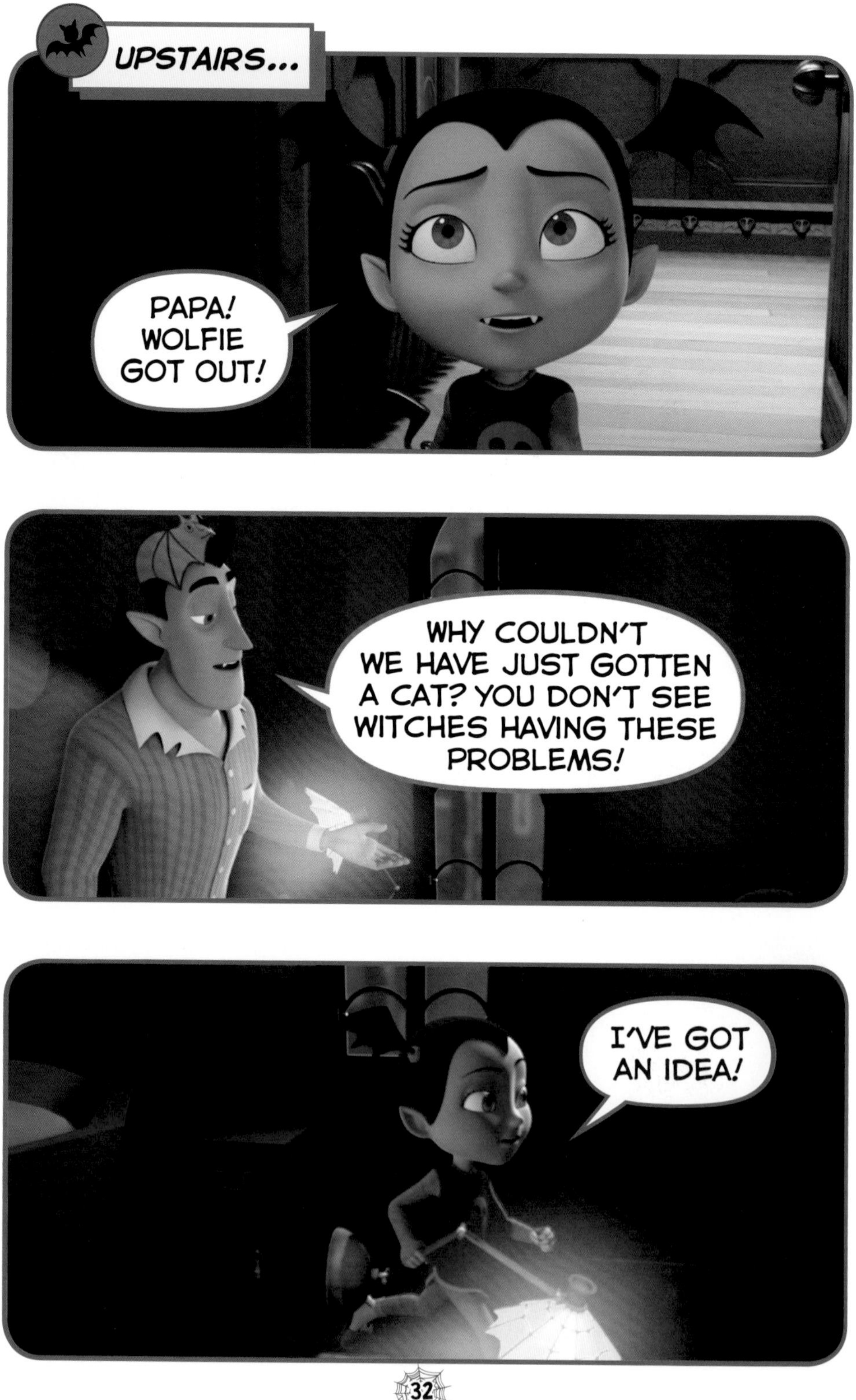
UPSTAIRS...
PAPA! WOLFIE GOT OUT!
WHY COULDN'T WE HAVE JUST GOTTEN A CAT? YOU DON'T SEE WITCHES HAVING THESE PROBLEMS!
I'VE GOT AN IDEA!

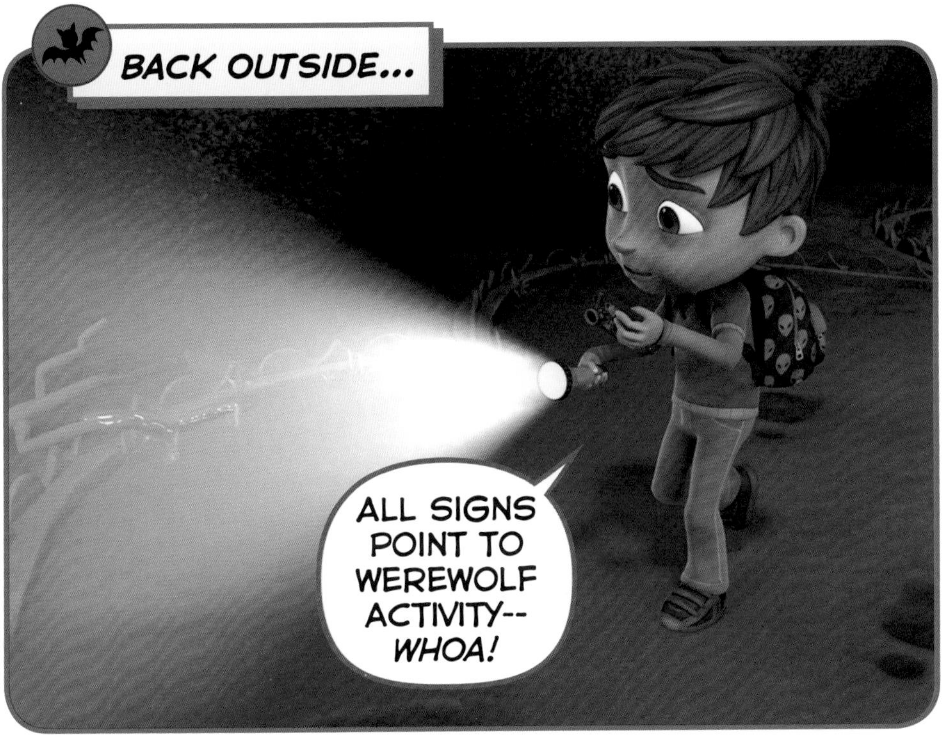
BACK OUTSIDE...
ALL SIGNS POINT TO WEREWOLF ACTIVITY-- *WHOA!*

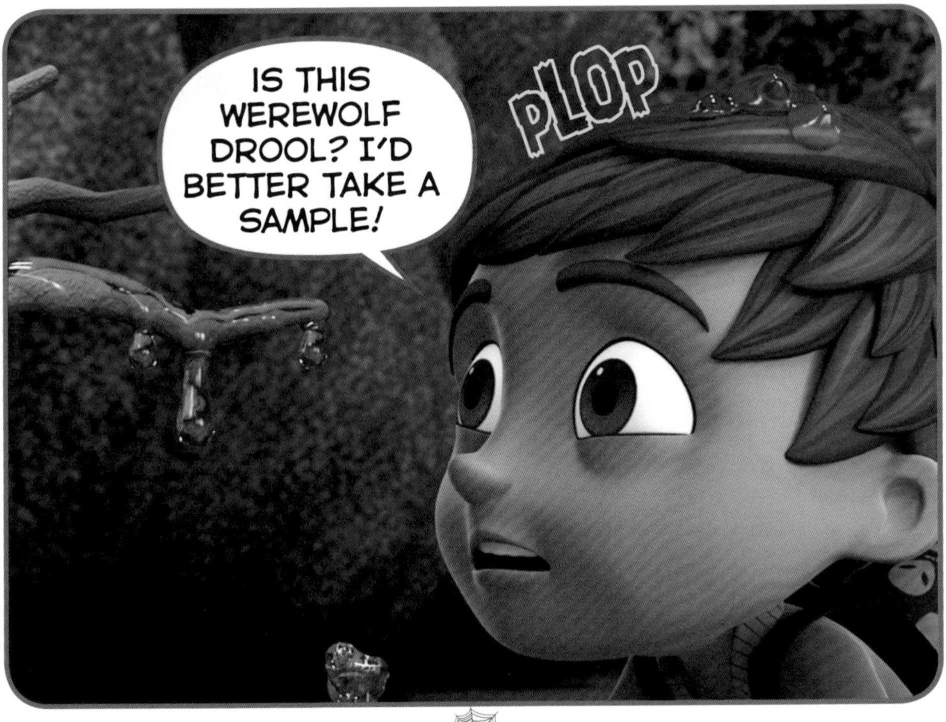
IS THIS WEREWOLF DROOL? I'D BETTER TAKE A SAMPLE!
PLOP

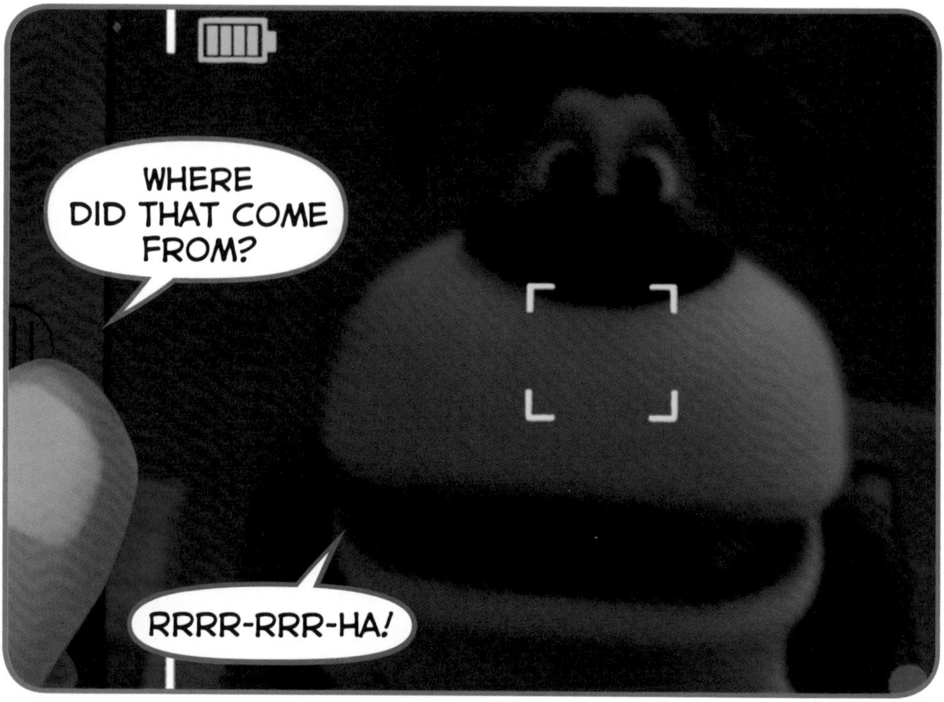
WHERE DID THAT COME FROM?
RRRR-RRR-HA!

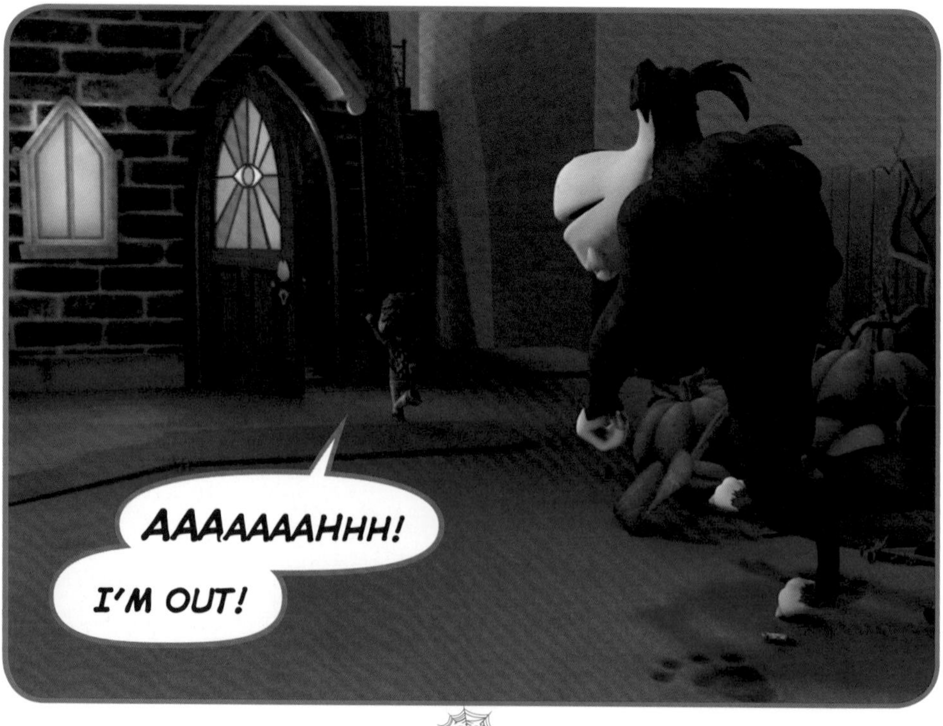
AAAAAAAHHH!
I'M OUT!

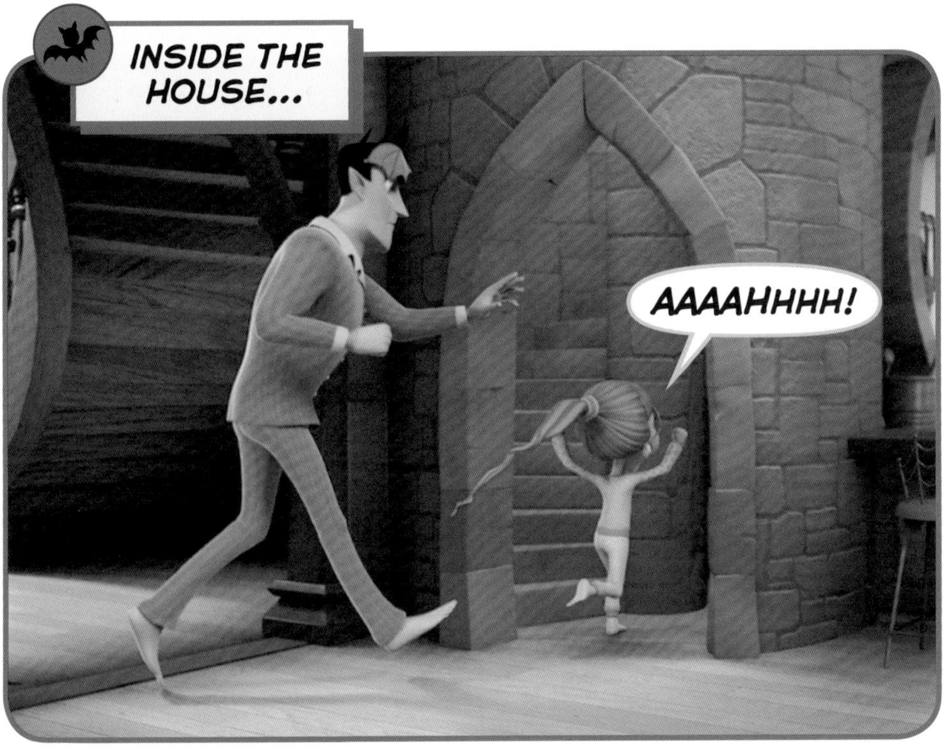
INSIDE THE HOUSE...
AAAAHHHH!

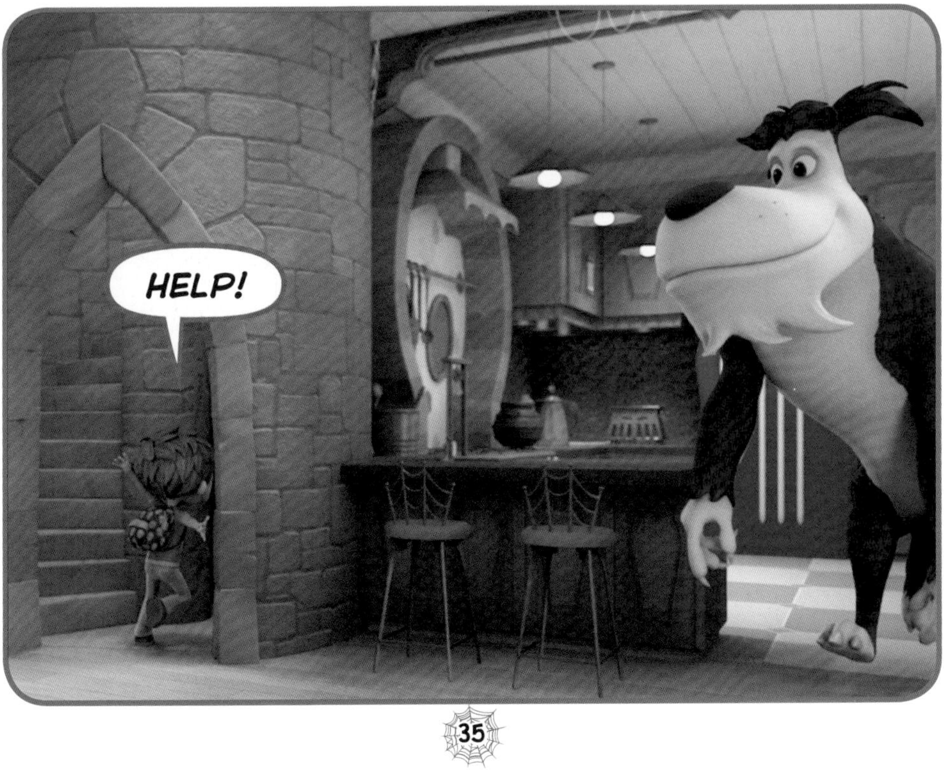
HELP!

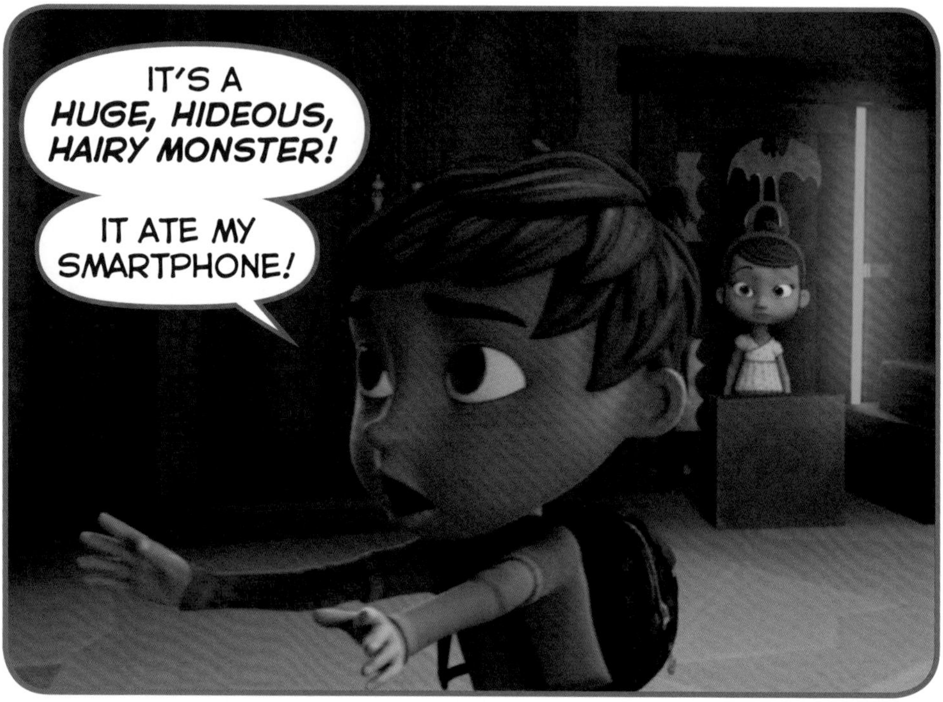
IT'S A *HUGE, HIDEOUS, HAIRY MONSTER!*
IT ATE MY SMARTPHONE!

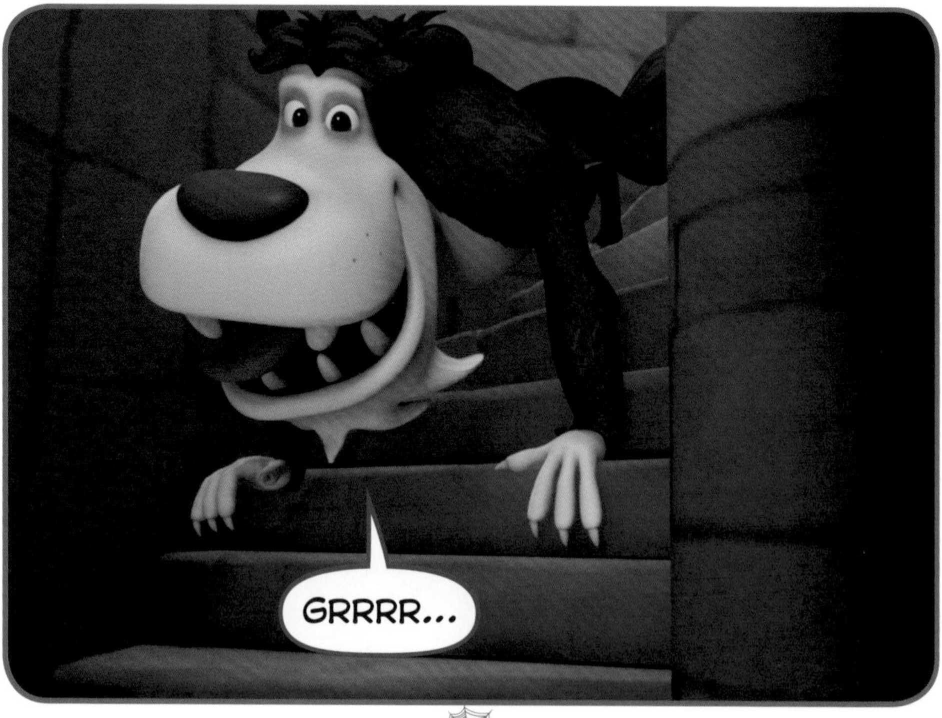
GRRRR...

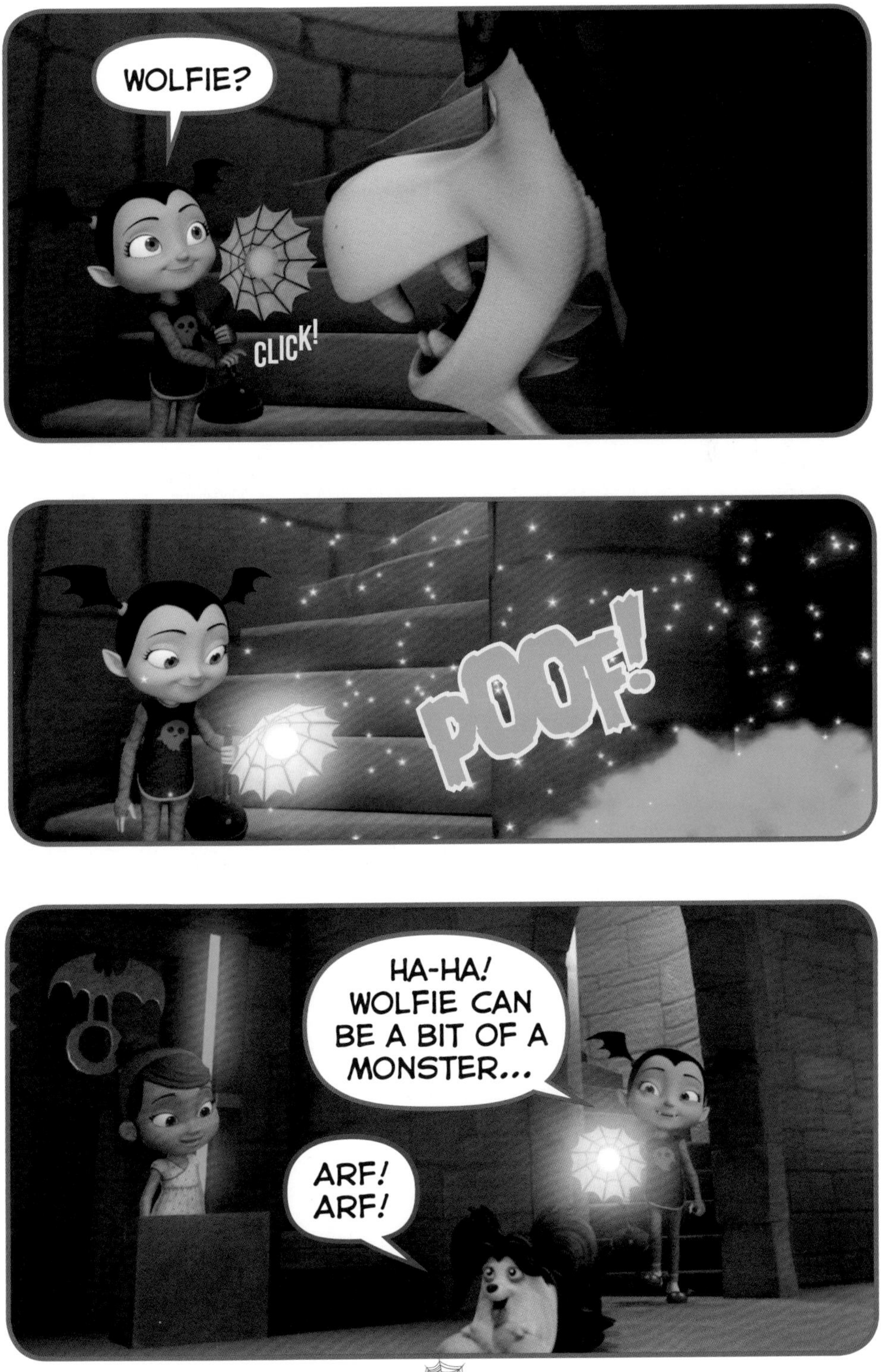
WOLFIE?
CLICK!
POOF!
HA-HA! WOLFIE CAN BE A BIT OF A MONSTER...
ARF! ARF!

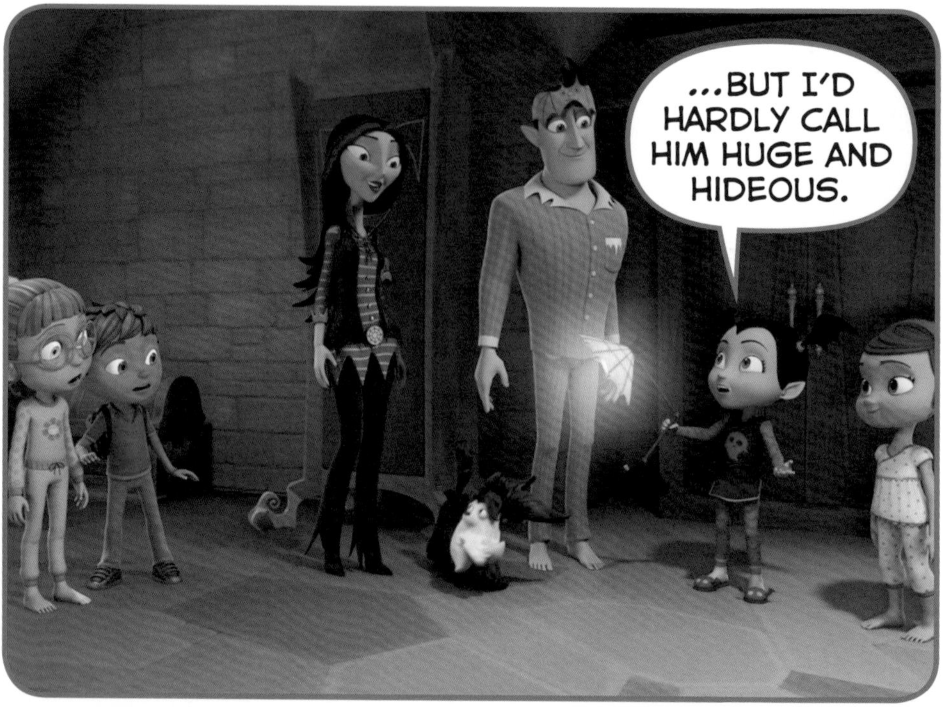
...BUT I'D HARDLY CALL HIM HUGE AND HIDEOUS.

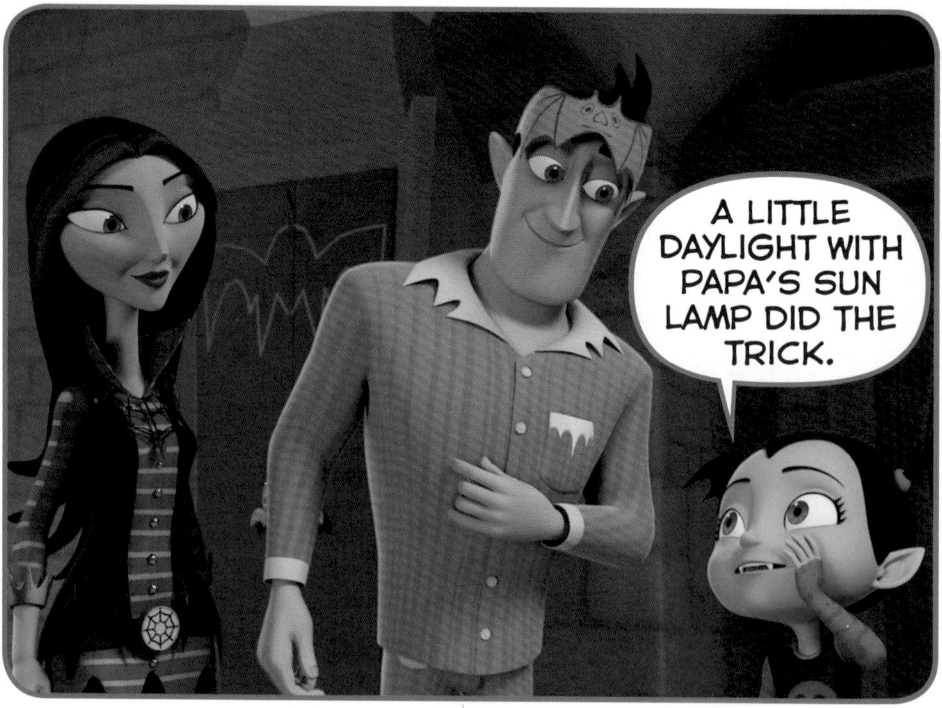
A LITTLE DAYLIGHT WITH PAPA'S SUN LAMP DID THE TRICK.

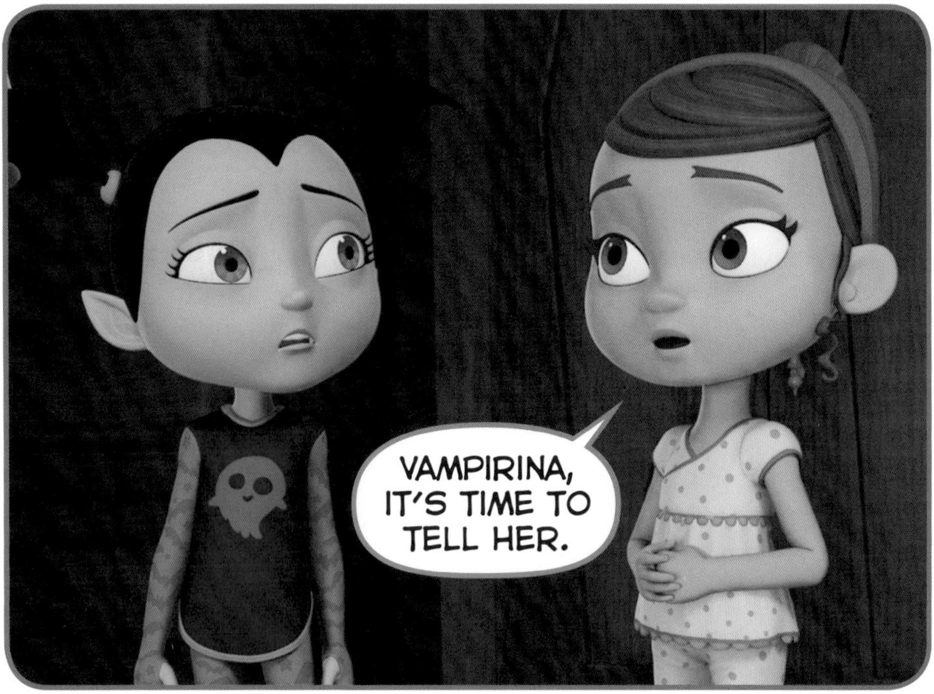
VAMPIRINA, IT'S TIME TO TELL HER.

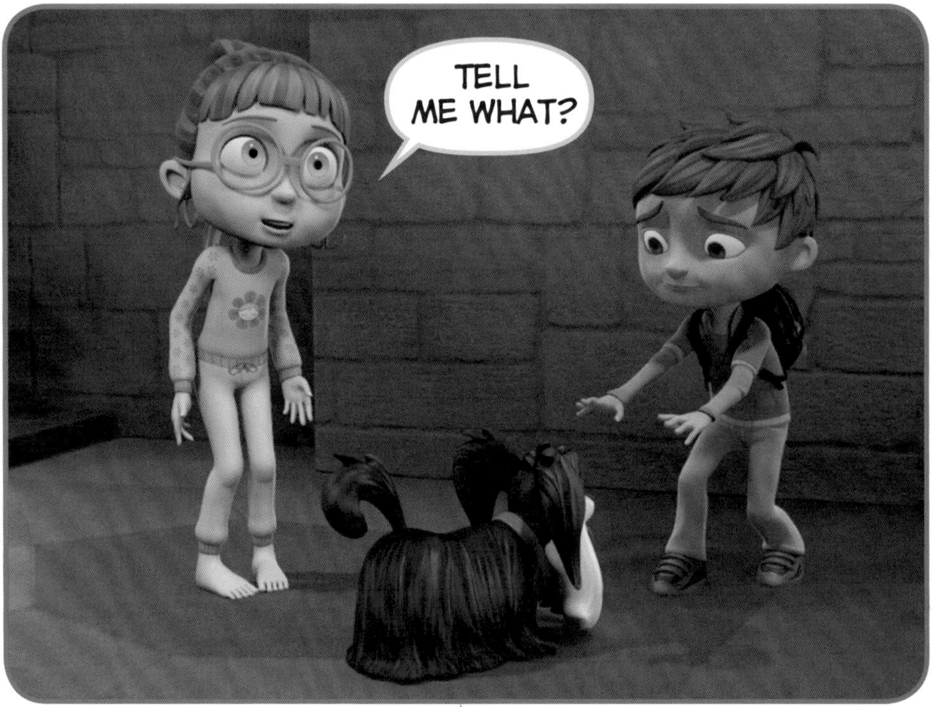
TELL ME WHAT?

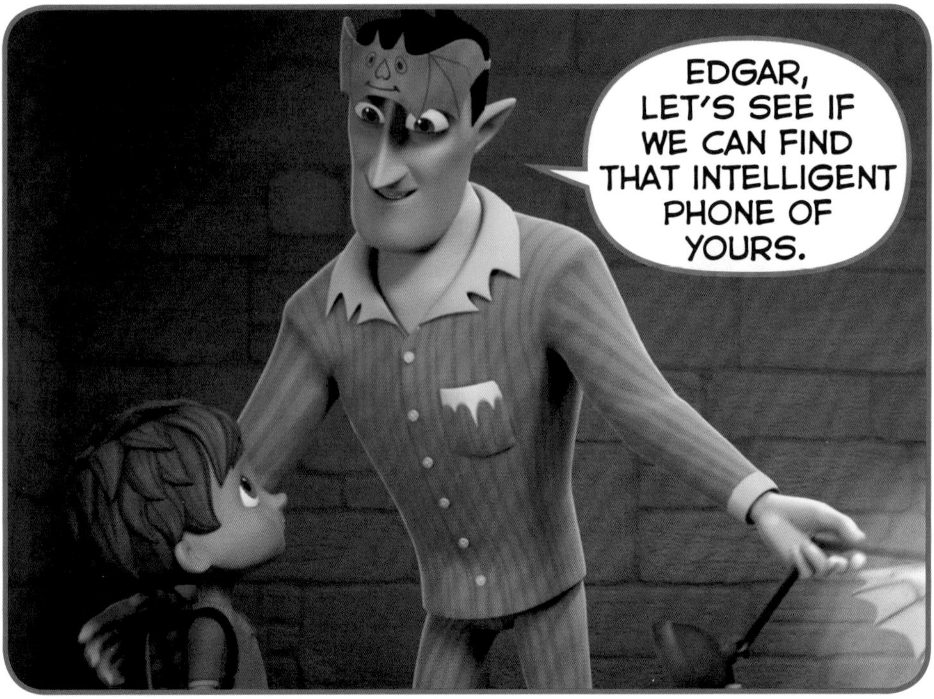
EDGAR, LET'S SEE IF WE CAN FIND THAT INTELLIGENT PHONE OF YOURS.

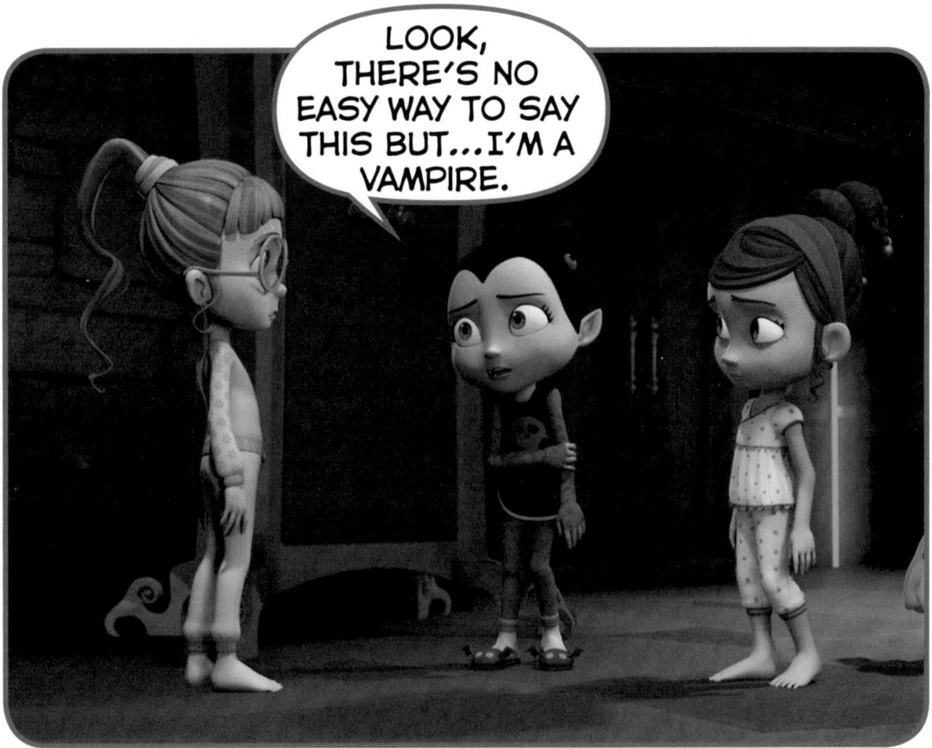
LOOK, THERE'S NO EASY WAY TO SAY THIS BUT...I'M A VAMPIRE.

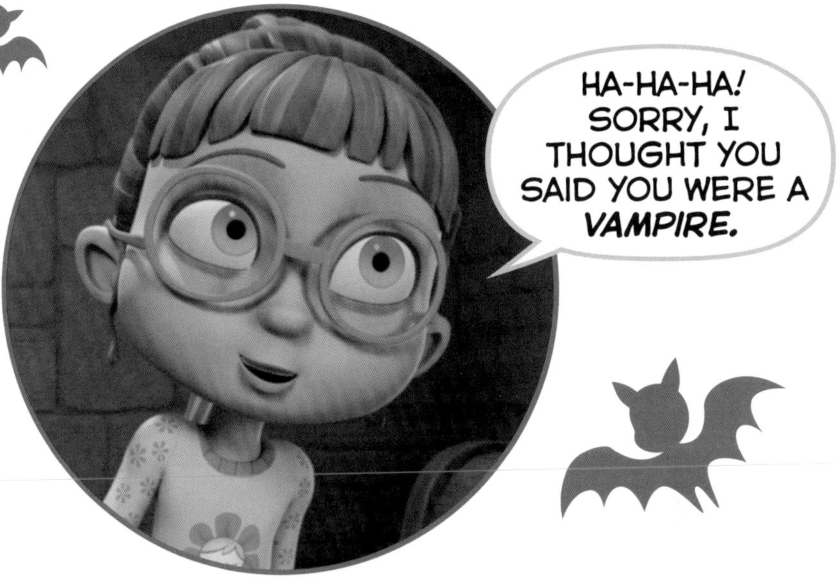
HA-HA-HA! SORRY, I THOUGHT YOU SAID YOU WERE A *VAMPIRE.*

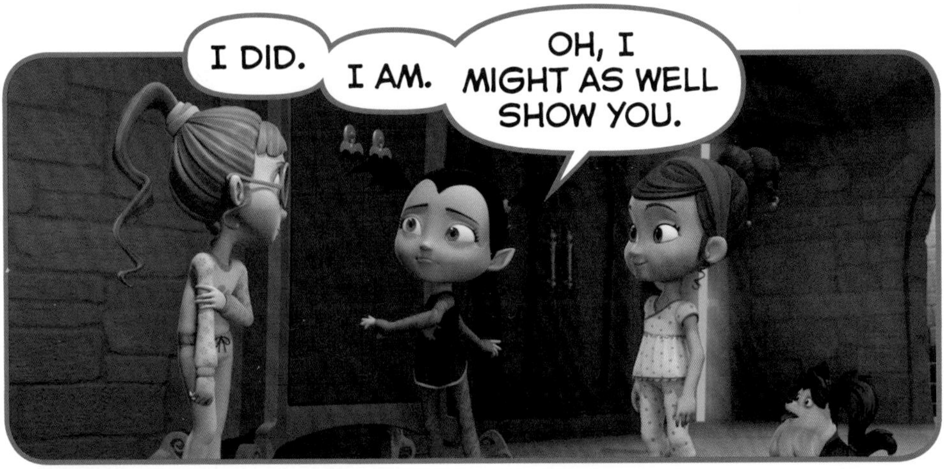
I DID.
I AM.
OH, I MIGHT AS WELL SHOW YOU.

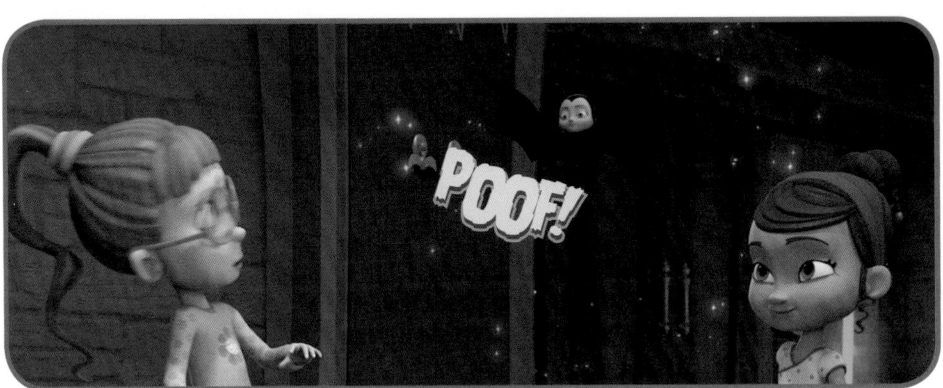
POOF!

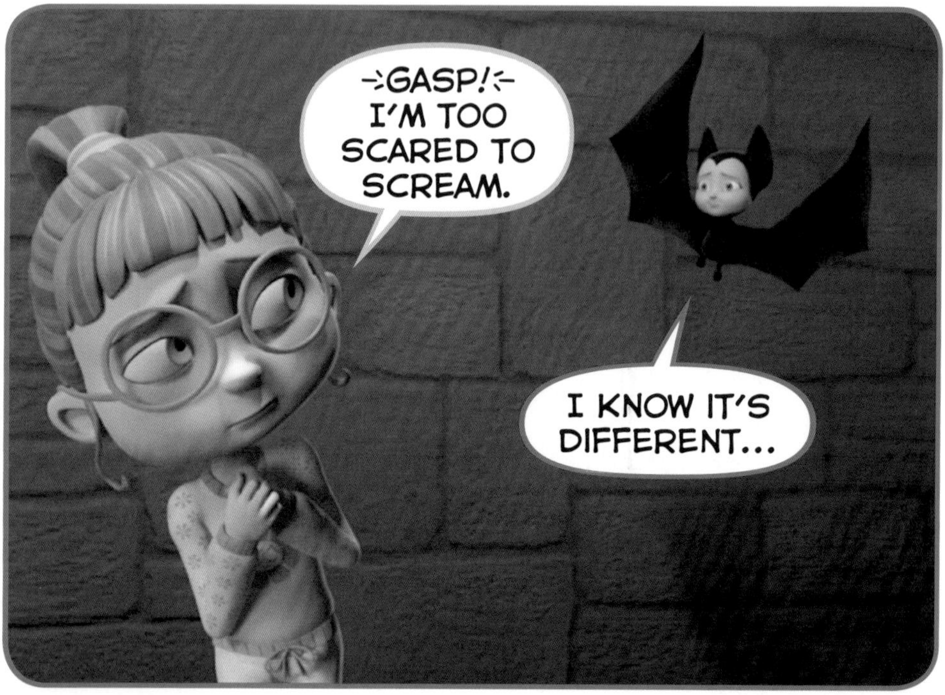
-GASP!- I'M TOO SCARED TO SCREAM.
I KNOW IT'S DIFFERENT...

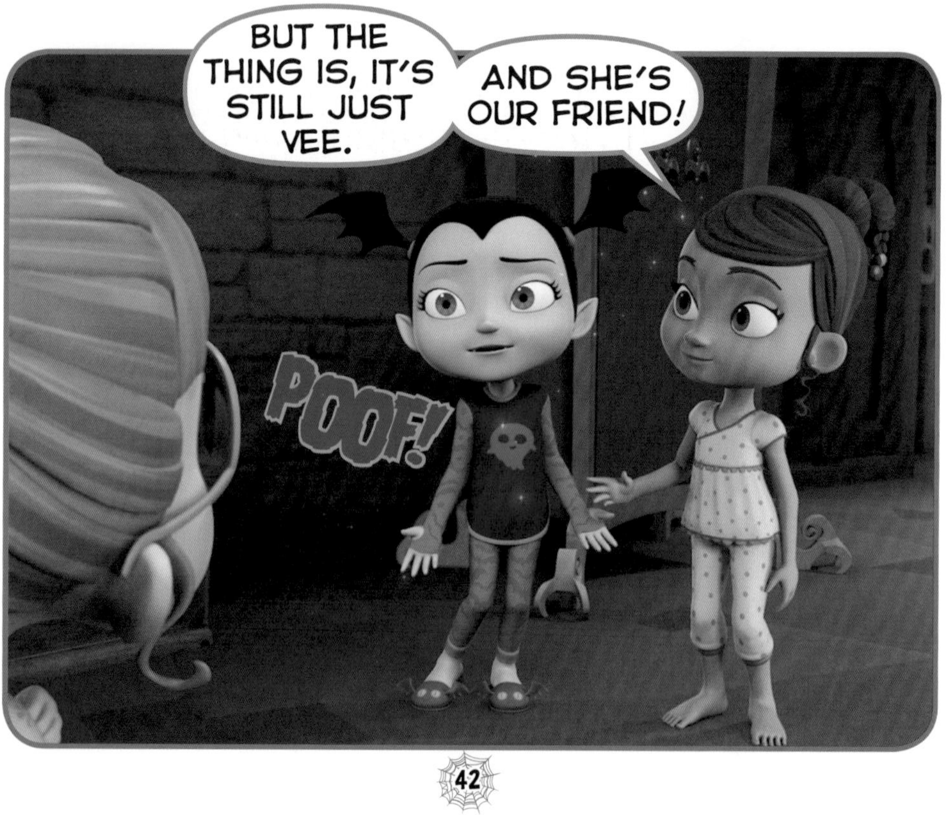
BUT THE THING IS, IT'S STILL JUST VEE.
AND SHE'S OUR FRIEND!
POOF!

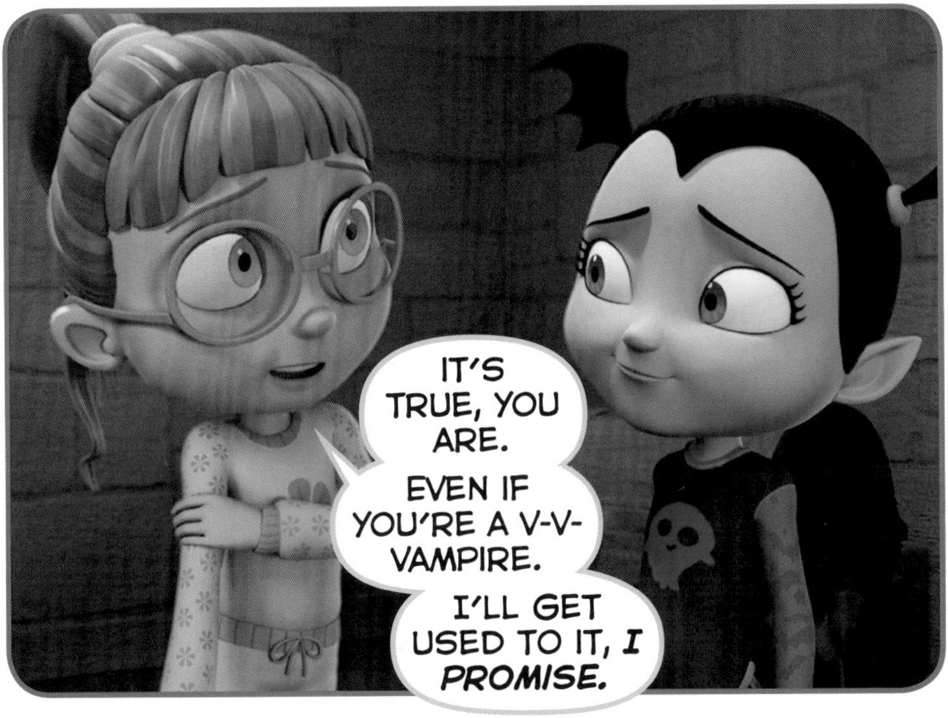
IT'S TRUE, YOU ARE.
EVEN IF YOU'RE A V-V-VAMPIRE.
I'LL GET USED TO IT, *I PROMISE.*

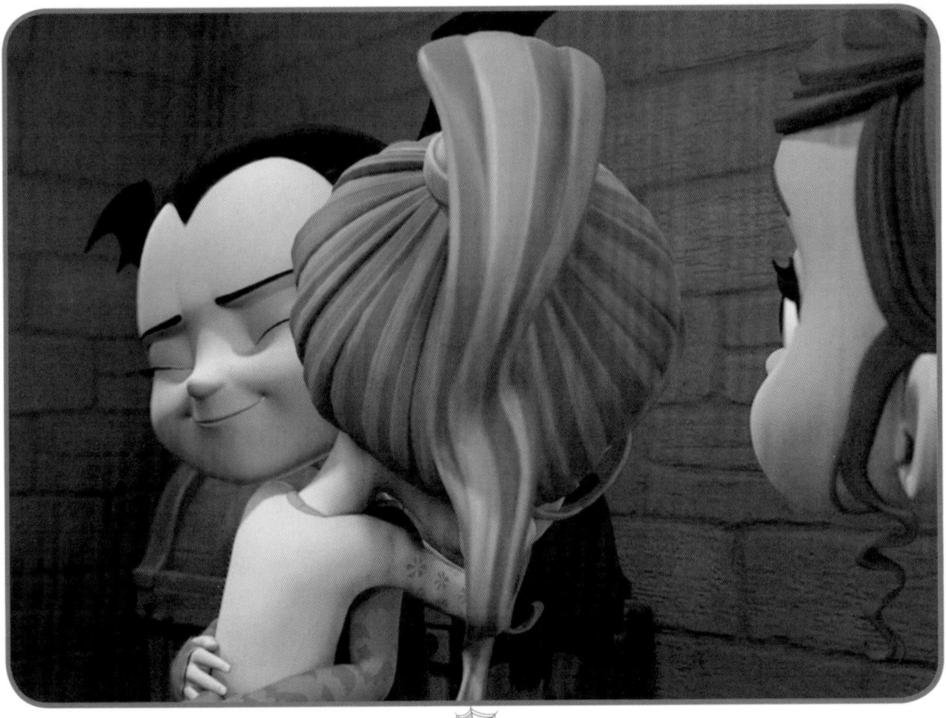

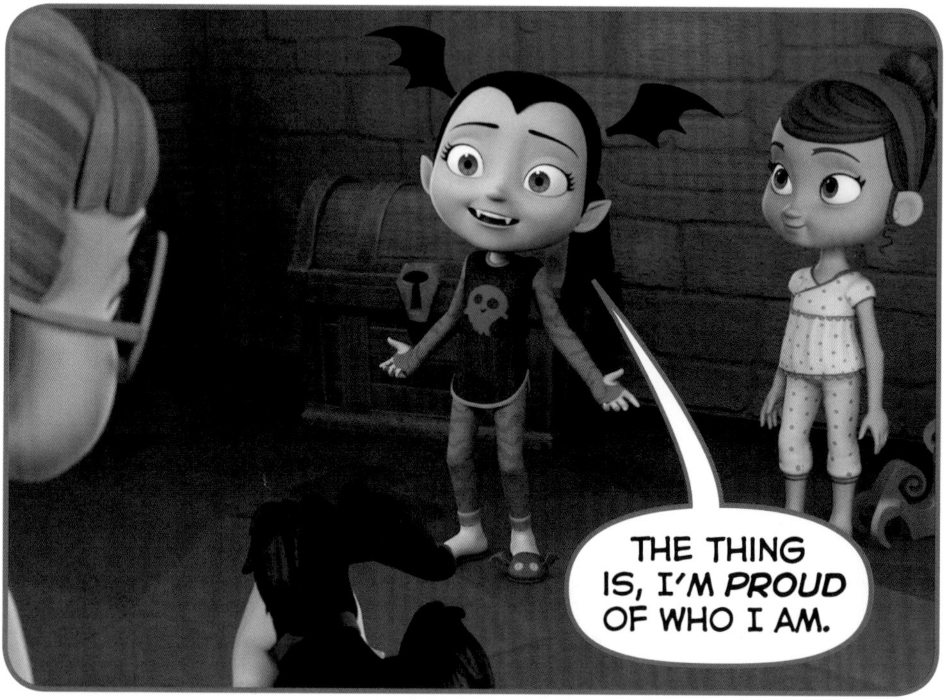
THE THING IS, I'M *PROUD* OF WHO I AM.

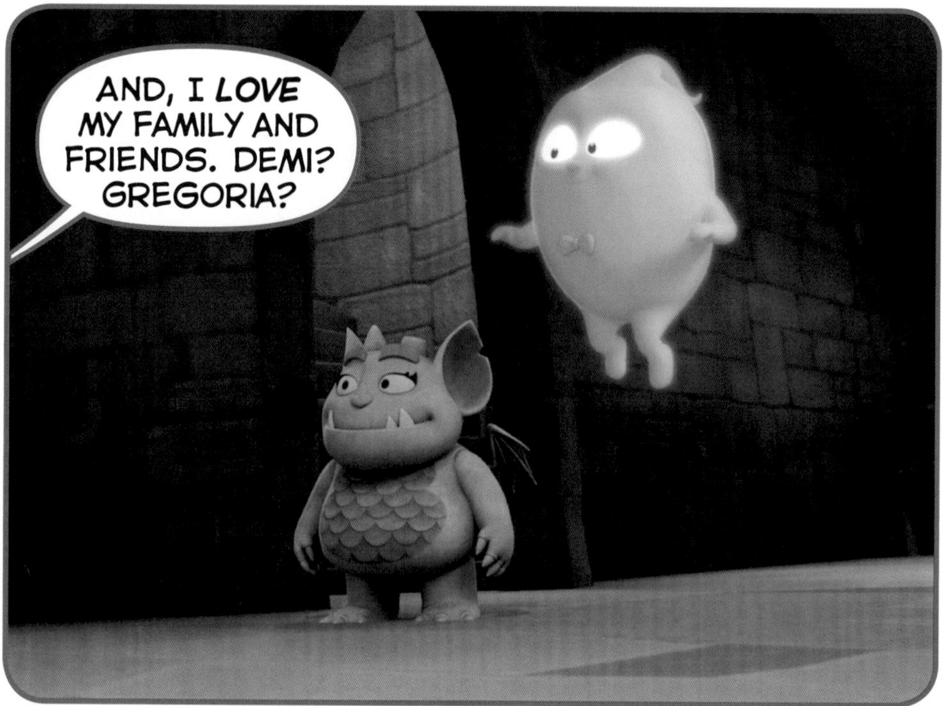
AND, I *LOVE* MY FAMILY AND FRIENDS. DEMI? GREGORIA?

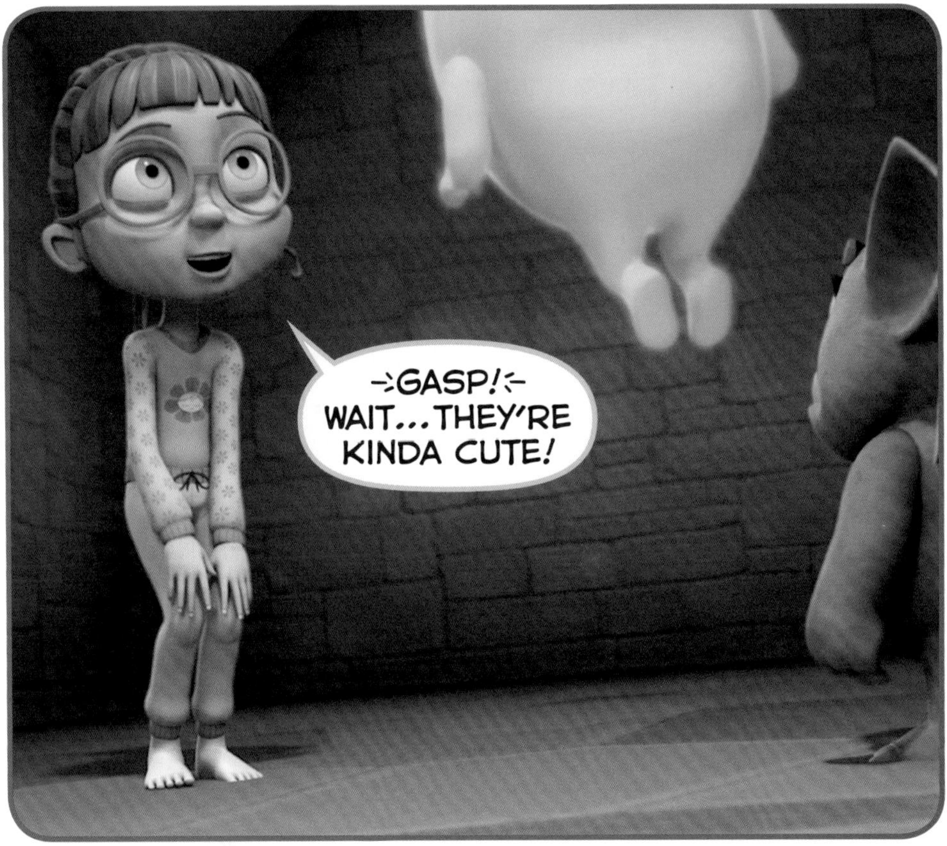
-GASP!-
WAIT...THEY'RE KINDA CUTE!

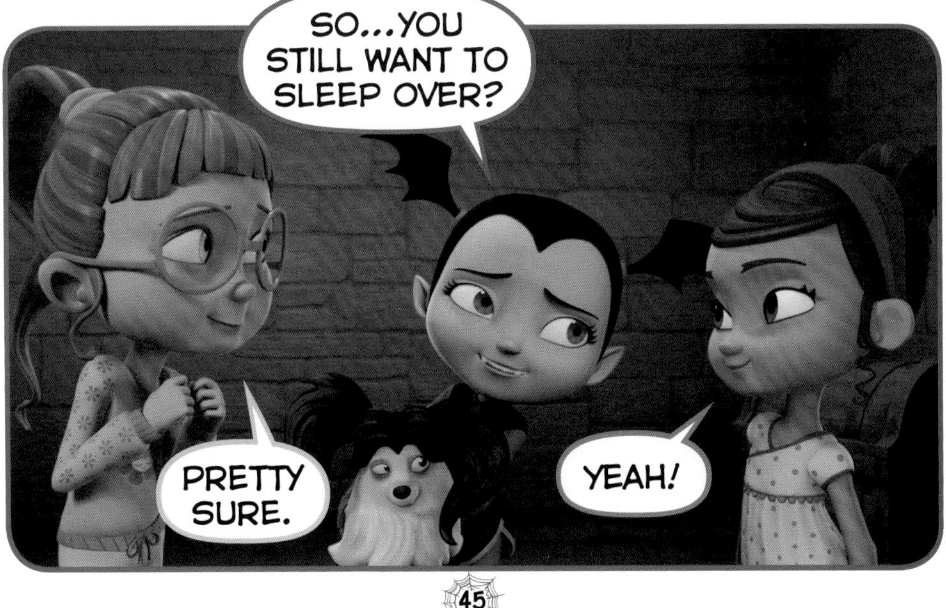
SO...YOU STILL WANT TO SLEEP OVER?
PRETTY SURE.
YEAH!

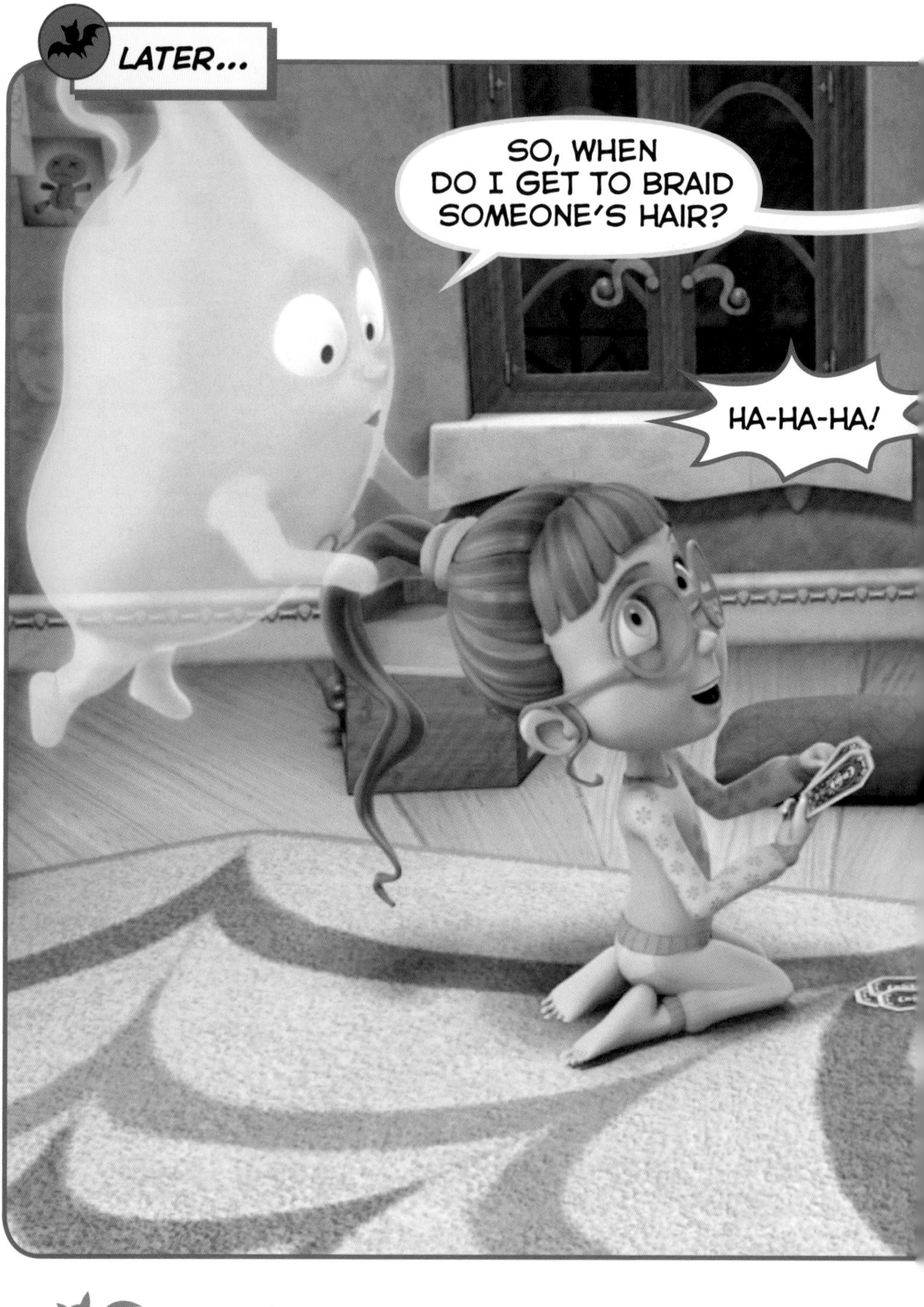
LATER...
SO, WHEN DO I GET TO BRAID SOMEONE'S HAIR?
HA-HA-HA!

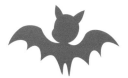

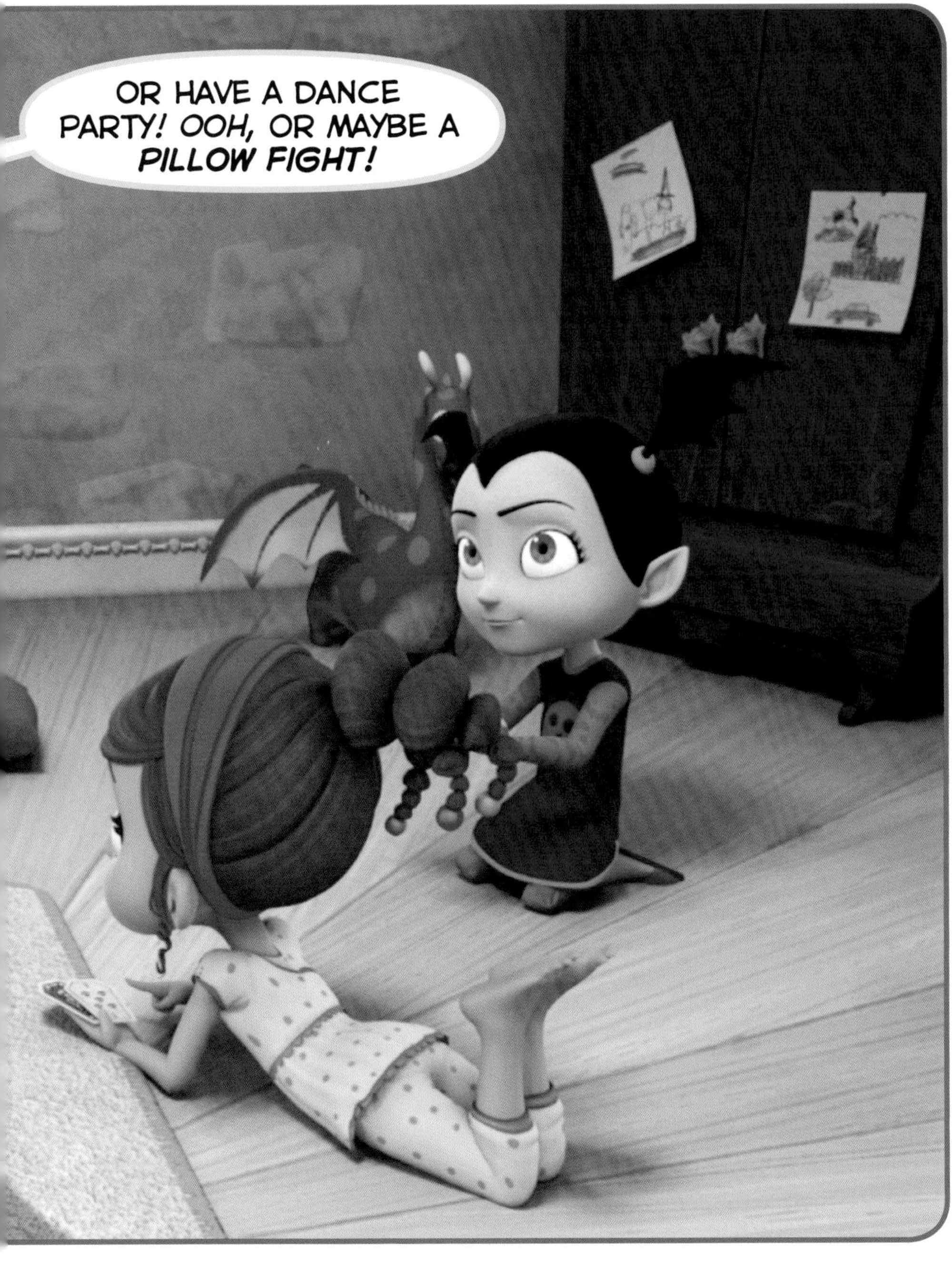
OR HAVE A DANCE PARTY! OOH, OR MAYBE A PILLOW FIGHT!

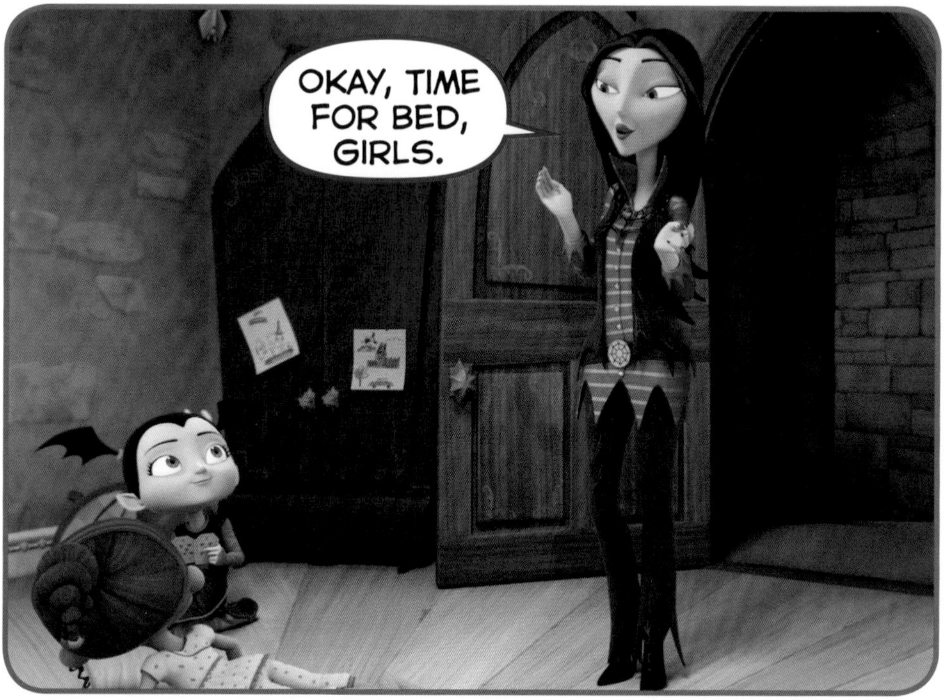
OKAY, TIME FOR BED, GIRLS.

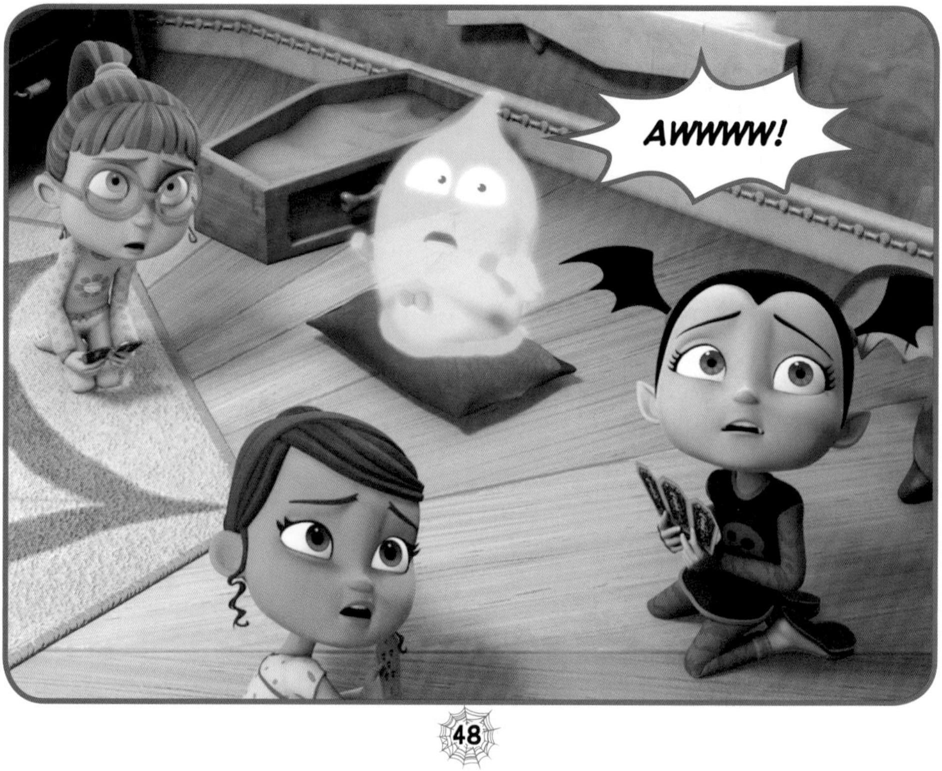
AWWWW!

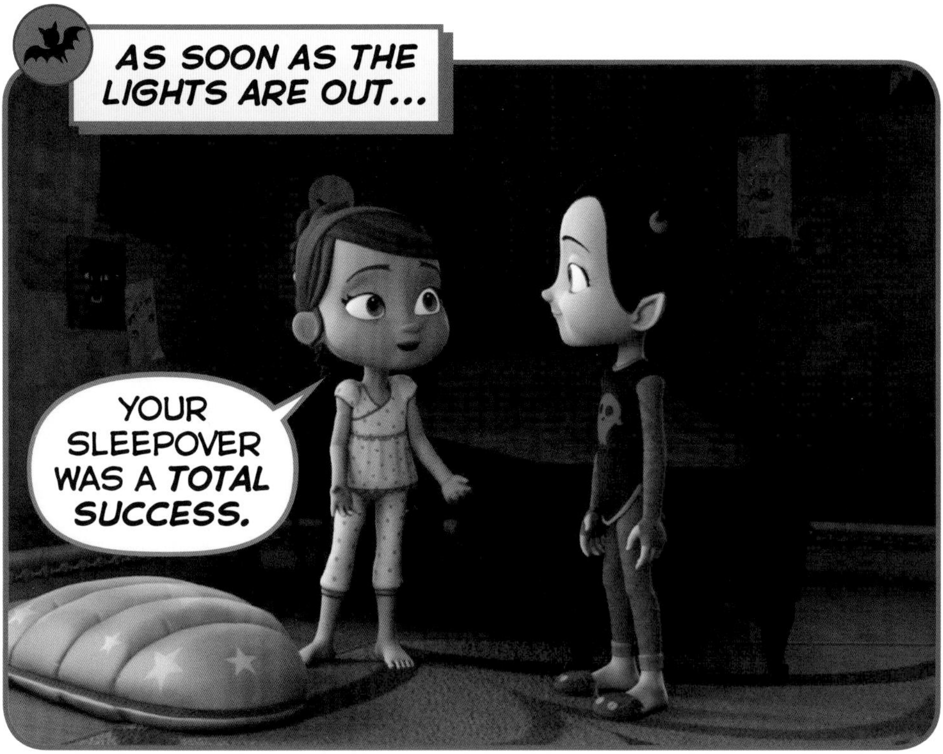
AS SOON AS THE LIGHTS ARE OUT...
YOUR SLEEPOVER WAS A *TOTAL SUCCESS.*

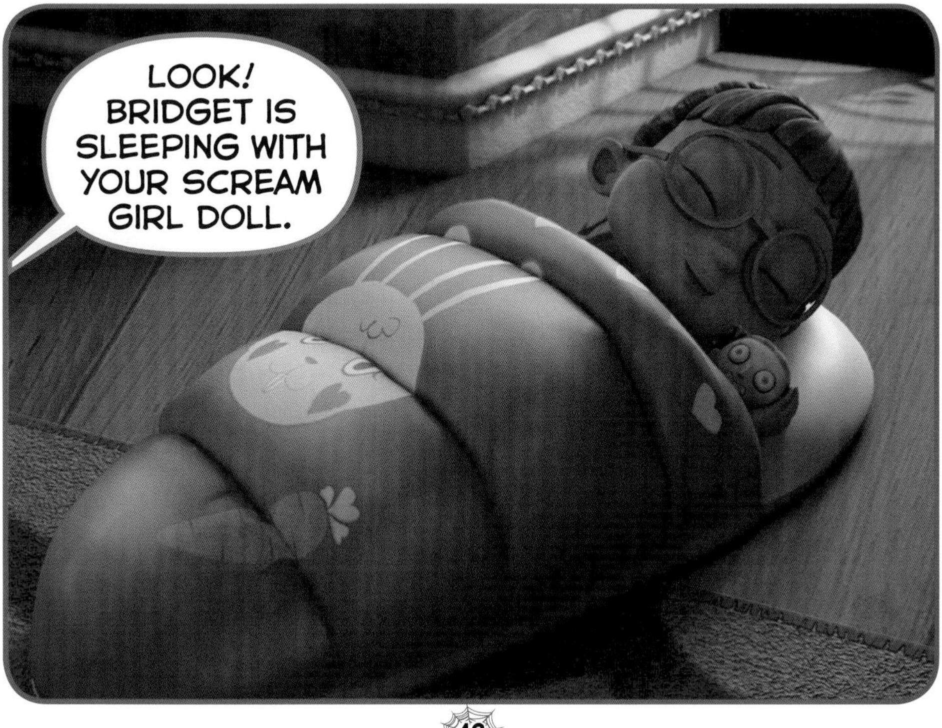
LOOK! BRIDGET IS SLEEPING WITH YOUR SCREAM GIRL DOLL.

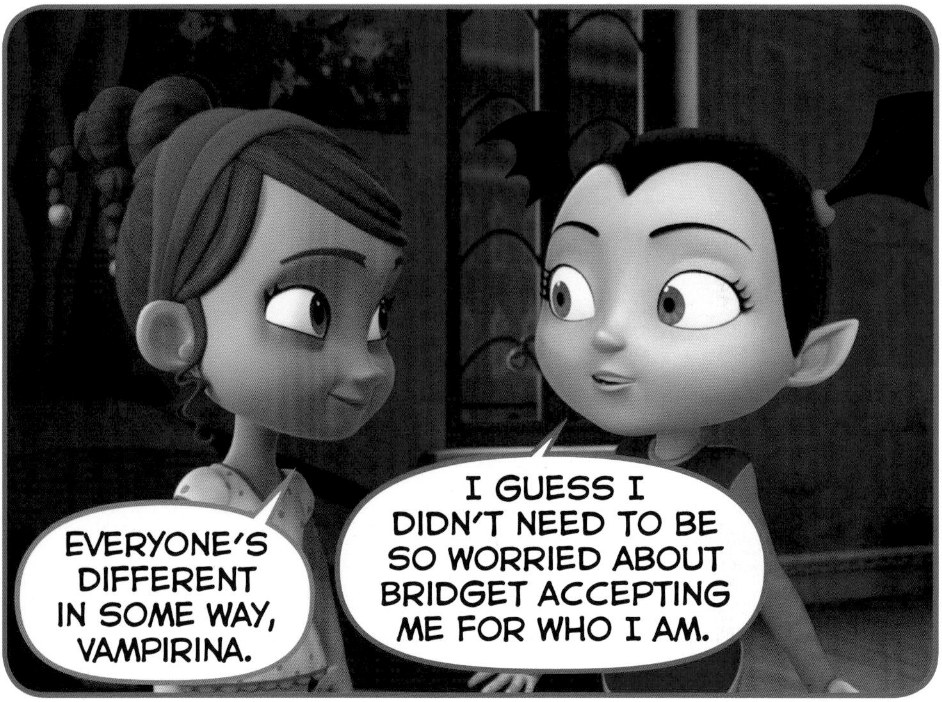
EVERYONE'S DIFFERENT IN SOME WAY, VAMPIRINA.
I GUESS I DIDN'T NEED TO BE SO WORRIED ABOUT BRIDGET ACCEPTING ME FOR WHO I AM.

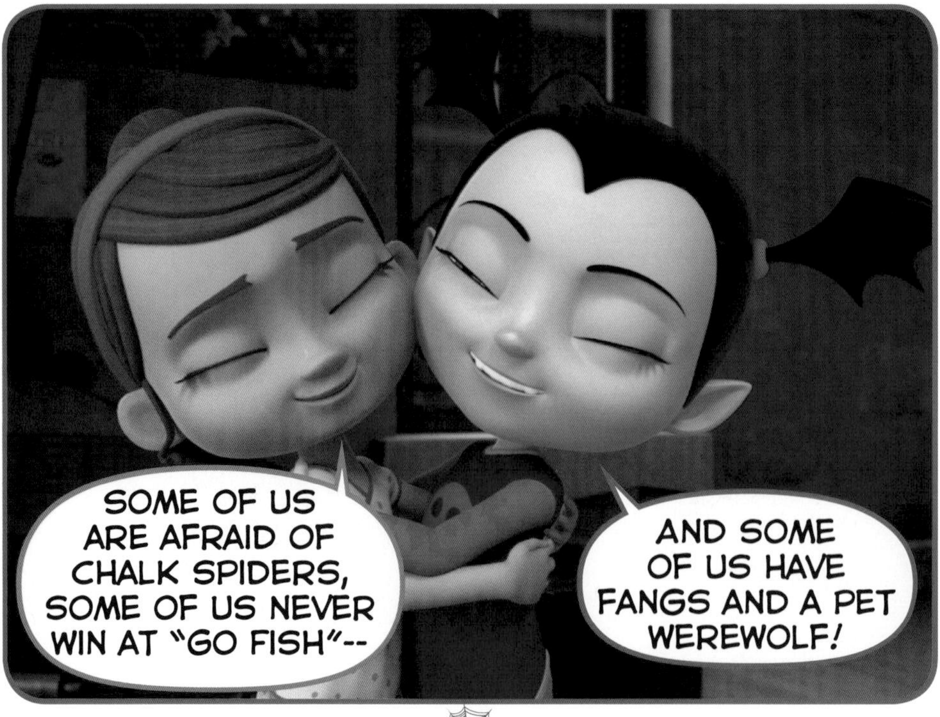
SOME OF US ARE AFRAID OF CHALK SPIDERS, SOME OF US NEVER WIN AT "GO FISH"--
AND SOME OF US HAVE FANGS AND A PET WEREWOLF!

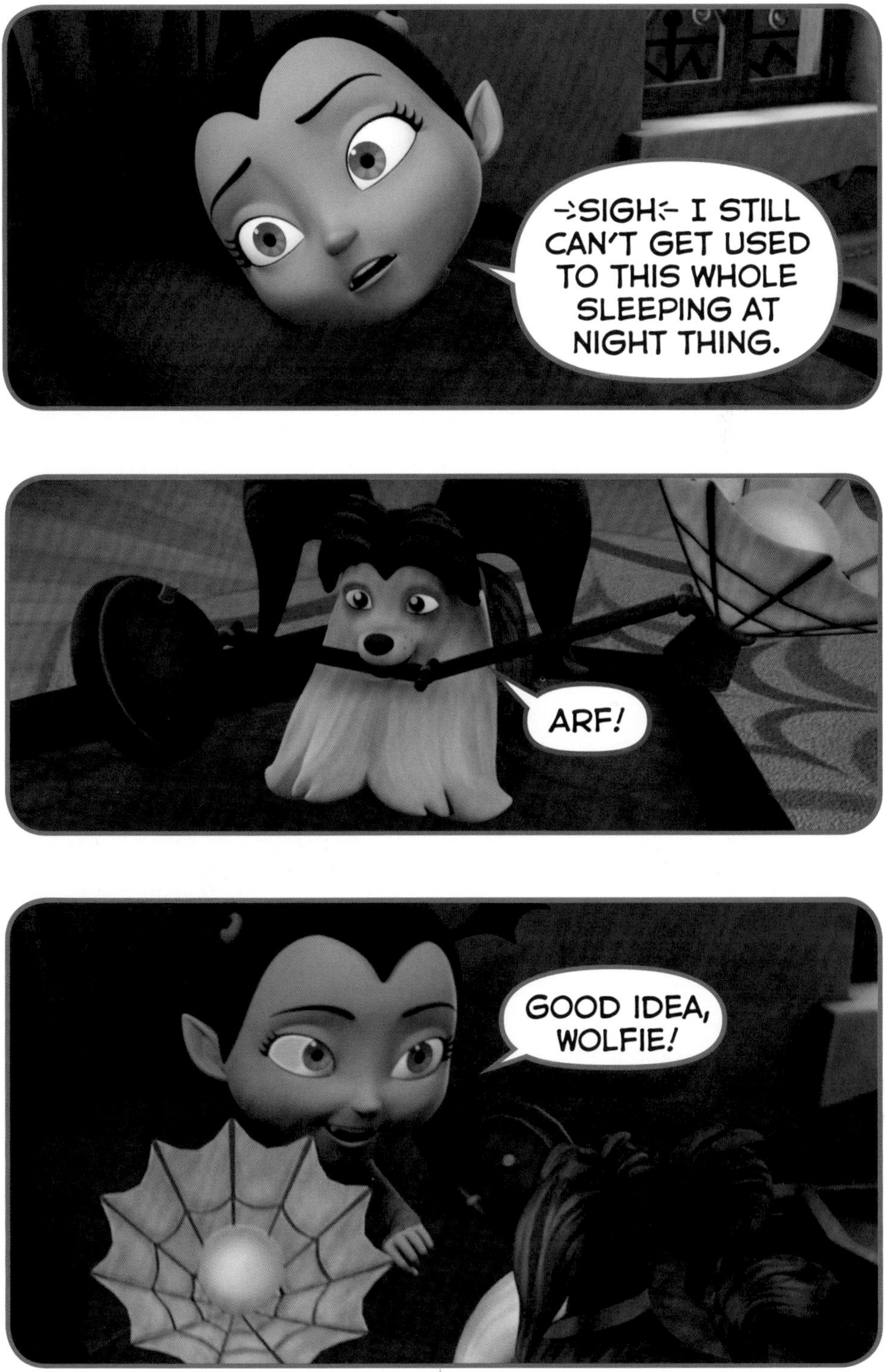
SIGH I STILL CAN'T GET USED TO THIS WHOLE SLEEPING AT NIGHT THING.
ARF!
GOOD IDEA, WOLFIE!

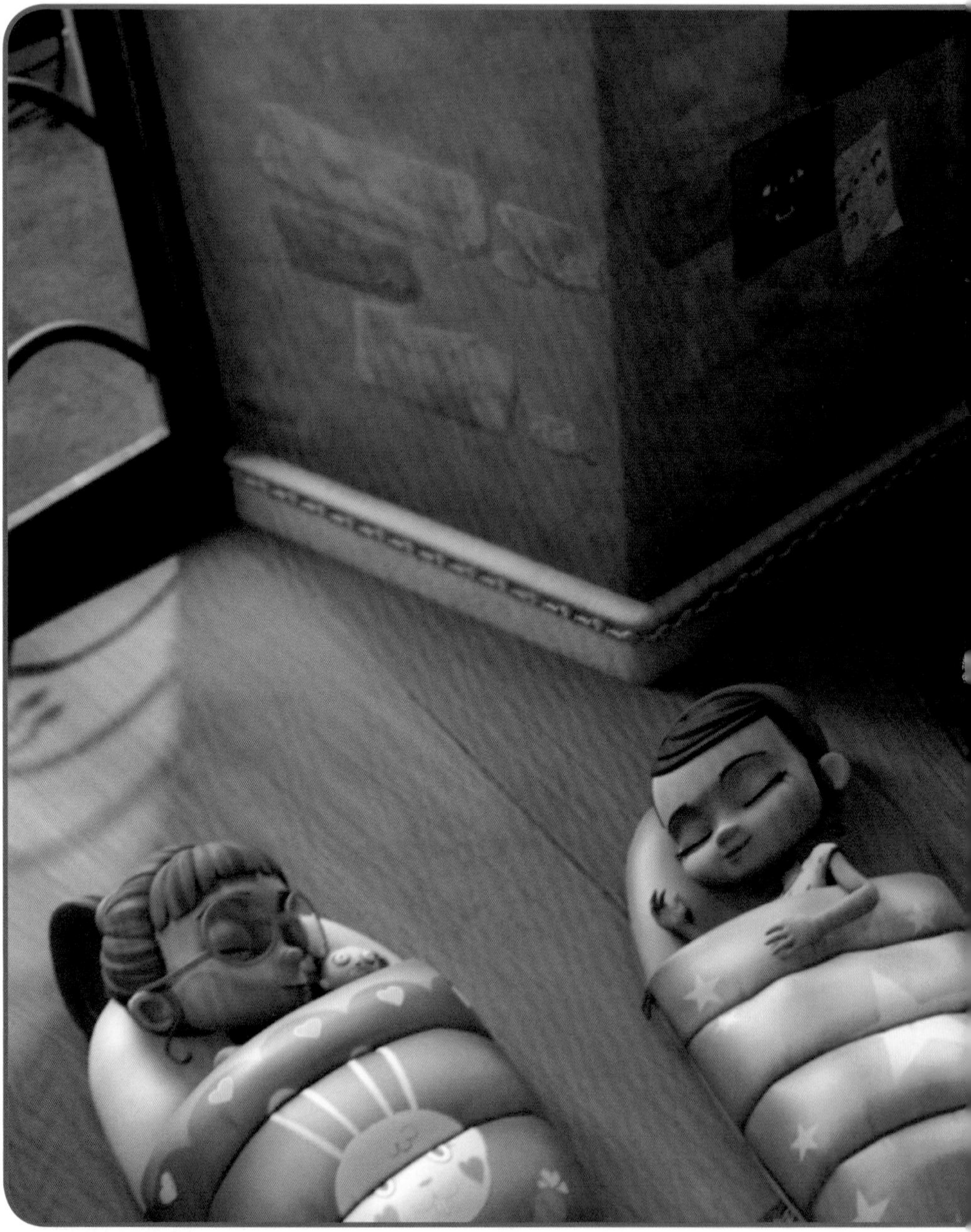

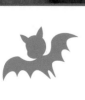

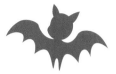

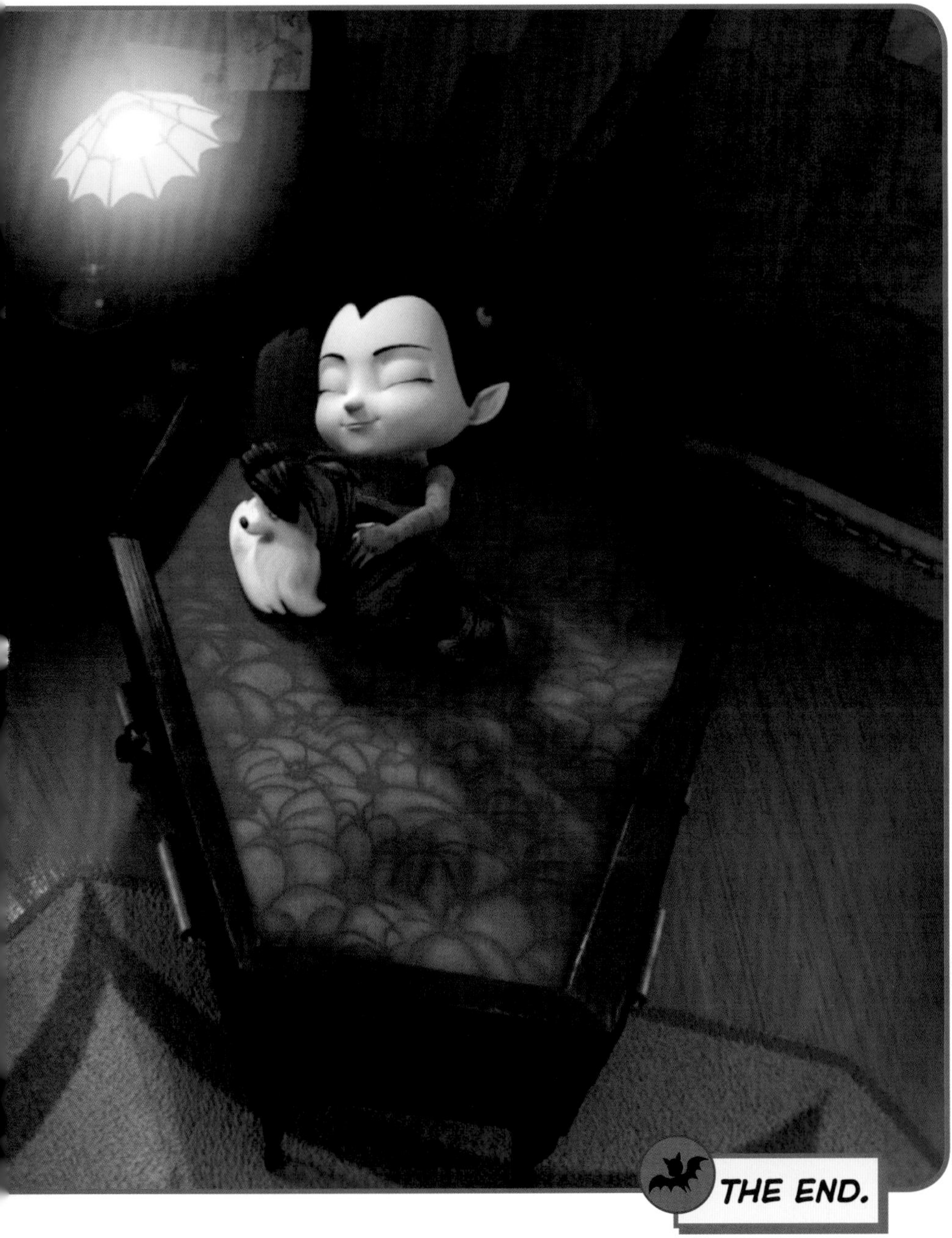
THE END.

"The Sleepover"

Based on the books written by Anne Marie Pace
and illustrated by LeUyen Pham

Developed for Television by
Chris Nee

Directed by
Nicky Phelan

Executive Producer and Story Editor
Chris Nee

Executive Producers
Cathal Gaffney
Darragh O'Connell

Written by
Chris Nee
Jeny Quine

Storyboard by
Charlie Grosvenor

CINESTORY COMIC

CINESTORY COMIC